DEVIL'S GOLD .

The forceful, bullying Joss Varney had wrecked Kelly's engagement and was now virtually keeping her a prisoner in his house on a remote part of the Californian coast. But what did he expect to get out of it, when it was so painfully clear that it was Damask Bentley who was really his kind of woman?

DEVIL'S GOLD

BY

NICOLA WEST

MILLS & BOON LIMITED
15–16 BROOK'S MEWS
LONDON W1A 1DR

First published 1982
Australiam copyright 1982
Philippine copyright 1982
This edition 1982

© *Nicola West 1982*

ISBN 0 263 74055 2

Set in Monophoto Plantin 11 on 12 pt.
01–1082

Made and printed in Great Britain by
Richard Clay (The Chaucer Press) Ltd,
Bungay, Suffolk

CHAPTER ONE

THE arrival lounge at San Francisco Airport was almost empty as Kelly's anxious green eyes scanned the few people left. Surely Mark would be along soon? What could have held him up?

Her heart quickened as a door swung open at the far end—but it wasn't Mark, she realised in disappointment. In fact, the man who came striding with the arrogant grace of a tiger into the lounge at that moment was about as different from her fiancé as it was possible to be. He moved as if he owned the entire airport, and even in the rough blue denims that he wore, she could see that his body must be as hard and fit as an athlete's, his broad shoulders stretching the faded shirt, his legs long and lean in the close-fitting jeans.

Fascinated, she watched as he came closer. He must be some kind of airport worker—nobody would come to meet a new arrival from London dressed like that. Anyway, he wasn't coming to meet *her*, thank goodness; the sheer blatant *maleness* that seemed to surround him like an aura would put her off at once. She preferred her men to be a little more civilised—like Mark.

Mark. Anxiety filled her as she glanced around. There was hardly anyone left now—and as her eyes came back to the tall, dark-haired man approaching her, she knew a quick stab of fear. Surely nothing could happen here, right in the airport lounge—even if this *was* America. But there was hardly anyone else about now—and he *was* heading straight for her. Suddenly scared, she threw him a wild glance and bent to pick up her luggage.

'I'll take the case.' The voice was hard and uncompromising, and she stifled a gasp as she looked up at him. He was right in front of her now, impossibly tall and broad, watching her with a dark, frowning glance. He held out his hand for the suitcase and, instinctively, she backed away, trembling, her nerves tingling with awareness.

'It's—it's all right,' she stammered, feeling her heart pound at his nearness. 'I—I'm being met. My fiancé——'

'I know all about that,' he cut in. 'Your fiancé's Mark Manners. And you're Kelly Francis—come all the way from little old England to be with him.' There was no mistaking the sneer in his voice, and she stared up at him, anger taking the place of her fear.

'Yes, I am—and what's wrong with that?' she demanded hotly. 'And just what business is it of yours anyway, Mr——?'

'I'm Joss Varney.' He bent and picked up the heaviest case as if it were a matchbox. 'Give me that other one too . . . I said, *give* it to me.' She passed it over without a word, and he caught her glance and grinned sardonically. 'No doubt you'll have heard of me.'

'Yes, I have.' Kelly had no choice but to fall into step beside him, but found that, even laden

with two heavy suitcases, his strides were so long
that she had almost to run to keep up with him.
'You're Mark's partner in—whatever it is you're
doing.' She allowed her voice to indicate how she
felt about that. 'Look, where *is* Mark? Why have
you come to meet me? I thought he'd be here—I
wired——'

'Well, of course you did, or I wouldn't be here,
would I?' He strode up to the self-opening doors,
which parted to let them through. 'My Chev's
parked over there, and the authorities don't allow
time for gossiping. There'll be time for questions
later.'

'But——' Kelly's protest was cut short as Joss
Varney suddenly dropped one of the cases and
grasped her arm in hard, cruel fingers, jerking her
back against him. Shocked and angry, she twisted
in his grip, then flinched as a large car swept past
only inches from the edge of the pavement. If Joss
hadn't been so quick, she would certainly have
been run down. She turned to thank him, but his
dark brown eyes mocked her as he released her
arm.

'We drive on the right here, in case you'd forgotten,' he drawled, and Kelly felt herself flush.
He needn't be so sarcastic about it! Rubbing her
arm, she followed silently as he led the way across
to the parking lot, not even bothering to look and
see if she was following. There'd been no need to
grab her like that, she told herself resentfully as
she scuttled after him. The man was altogether
too pleased with himself, and rude and overbear-

ing into the bargain. And just what *had* happened to prevent Mark coming to meet her himself?

It was all so different from what she had pictured. She had spent the whole journey visualising their reunion—the way Mark's face would light up when he saw her, the way she would fling herself into his arms, their first kiss ... And instead there was this—this obnoxious man, who wouldn't even wait for her to keep up!

And now—why, he was stopping beside a battered old Chevrolet truck, swinging her cases into the cluttered back. Surely he didn't expect her to ride in *that*! Why, it was filthy, covered in reddish mud. Desperately she glanced around, hoping that even now by some miracle Mark would appear and whisk her away with him. But the whole place seemed deserted. Apart from a small bunch of people waiting at a bus stop for their hotel transport, there was nobody in sight. Certainly nobody who would think there was anything incongruous in the sight of Kelly Francis getting into a dirty old truck with a man she'd never met before and hated on sight. . . .

It seemed, Kelly thought resignedly, that she had no alternative, and she clambered up into the passenger seat, receiving no help—naturally—from her companion. What a brute he was, she thought, settling into the hard seat. How could Mark have ever taken up with such a boor? It merely confirmed the suspicions she had had ever since Mark wrote to tell her he was leaving Seattle—that he had got mixed up with an adventurer, a con-man, someone who would use him and his small capital for his own ends and eventually, having bled him white, leave him for fresh game.

Joss Varney didn't spare her a glance as he thrust the Chev into gear and drove out of the airport. Once again, Kelly knew a rush of panic as she realised that nobody knew where she was—not even Mark, perhaps, for she had only this man's word for it that Mark had sent him here.

A dark fear gripped her as she thought of all the things that might have happened. After all, she had no reason to trust this man—even at a distance of nine thousand miles, the name Joss Varney had given her cause for nothing but suspicion. And here she was, going off with him heaven knew where in a battered old Chevrolet that surely wouldn't have passed any M.O.T. back home. . . .

She stole a glance at the stern profile. He was at least twice her size. The tautness of his blue denim shirt betrayed the broad, powerful shoulders above equally muscular arms revealed by rolled-up sleeves. His hands on the steering wheel were lean, yet strong enough, she thought, to strangle a lion. . . . A tiny sob rose in her throat, and although Joss Varney seemed to be intent on the road he caught the sound and gave her a quick glance.

'For God's sake,' he said impatiently, 'there's nothing to be scared of. I'm not going to drag you behind a bush and rape you! I don't go in for

cradle-snatching. I just want to get out of this
damned city and back on the road to camp before
it gets dark. As it is, we'll have to stop for a meal
on the way.' He swung the truck round a bend.
'You do eat, I take it?'

'You don't have to worry about me,' Kelly said
grandly. 'I had a meal on the plane. And I don't
like to eat too much.'

'No, I can see that.' He turned his head and his
gaze raked her slight body, its slenderness emphasised by cream linen slacks and pink shirt.
'You don't look as if you eat enough to keep a
sparrow alive. One of these slimming fanatics, I
guess.'

The contempt in his voice stung her and she
retorted: 'Certainly not! I simply happen to believe one doesn't need to be a glutton to survive.'

'Bully for you,' he answered, and now his voice
was maddeningly indifferent. Shrugging with
annoyance, Kelly turned to look out of her
window—and couldn't repress a gasp of delight.

So far they had been travelling along a busy
freeway and she hadn't paid much attention to
what lay beyond. Now she saw that they were
approaching a bridge—a bridge so long that its
other end was lost in the pearly mist of late afternoon, while beneath it the sea danced in blue
waves flecked with glittering white foam and sailing boats swooped like gulls, their sails billowing
and multi-coloured against the eggshell-blue
spring sky.

'This isn't the Golden Gate, is it?' she asked,

forgetting her antagonism for a moment.

Joss Varney didn't even take his eyes from the road ahead as he answered curtly: 'No. This is the Bay Bridge. It's a sight longer'n the Golden Gate—that spans the Bay entrance. That's San Francisco behind to your left, if you're interested, and Oakland ahead.'

If she was interested! Kelly twisted round to look behind her and gasped again at the beauty of the skyline and waterfront. She had been looking forward to exploring San Francisco, and enjoying the sights she had heard so much about— Fisherman's Wharf, the cable cars that climbed 'half-way to the stars', Chinatown. ... But it looked as if she was not to be allowed even one evening there. And once again the thought of Mark came to her mind, and her fears returned.

'Look, Mr Varney,' she began with a bravado she didn't feel, 'don't you think it's time you answered a few questions? Like where's Mark, and where are you taking me? And just what all this is about?'

The searing glance raked her again, leaving her feeling small and helpless. Just what was it about this man that had the effect of reducing her to jelly? And why should she stand for it? But even as she opened her mouth again, he cut in harshly and silenced her protests.

'I told you—time for questions later. And if you and I are going to spend any time at all together— which I can't see any alternative for, worse luck— there's just a few things you're going to have to learn about me. One is, I don't like chattering women with me while I'm driving. And another is, I don't like chattering women, period. Got it?' He glanced at her and seemed to gain satisfaction from her stunned silence. 'Right. So we understand each other, yeah?'

Kelly spluttered and found her voice. 'We understand each other, *no*, Mr Varney! And you can rest assured that I don't want us to spend time together any more than you do! So since the whole thing's so repulsive to you, you can just put me down at the next taxi-rank we come to, tell me where Mark is, and I'll get the rest of the way by myself! Got *that*?'

'Nothing,' he said with heavy irony, 'would give me greater pleasure—*Miss* Francis. Unfortunately, I'm just not able to carry out your orders just at this moment. So I guess we're stuck with each other. And now you can button up those pretty little lips and be quiet. You may not have noticed it, but there's one hell of a lot of traffic around on these roads at this time of day. I need all my concentration for that.'

Kelly subsided. It was true that the traffic was heavy on the bridge and through Oakland, which she guessed to be the next stretch of city they passed through. She peered from the window, noticing the many differences in the American street—the rows of motels and restaurants, the hoardings, the traffic lights strung across the road. She thought ruefully of how she had looked forward to this first sight of America, and even in her present state of mind she couldn't help feeling a surge of excitement at the thought that at last she was here—in California—seeing things she had heard of but never thought to see for herself. And never would, she reminded herself, if it hadn't been for her anxiety over Mark.

Beside her, Joss Varney muttered something and swung the Chev off the road. Kelly looked up in alarm and saw that they were stopping in the car park of a restaurant. She turned as Joss switched off the engine.

'I told you, you don't need to bother about me——'

'No, I know you don't need food to survive.' He reached across her to unfasten the door and his arm brushed across her breasts, setting up a tingle that spread through her whole body. 'But I do. And I warn you, I eat a lot. So if you don't like the idea of watching the pigs feed, don't come in. It's all one to me.' He swung himself out of his own seat and came round to look up at her. 'But I shan't be stopping again, and there's damn little food in camp, so unless you want to go on a fast I'd advise you to come in, and have a cup of coffee at least.'

He was walking away before she could answer, complete indifference expressed in the set of his broad, muscular back. Kelly bit her lip and tensed her body in an attempt to control the unaccountable shivering that had started up. Maybe a cup of coffee would be a good idea after all; it was some time now since that rather plastic meal on the plane. And she was feeling oddly tired. Though that wasn't so very odd, she told herself as she scrambled awkwardly down from the Chev, thankful that she had taken a friend's advice and worn comfortable trousers for the flight; after all, it was now past midnight at home and she hadn't slept at all on the plane.

Joss Varney was already seated when she entered the restaurant, looking hesitantly about her. A smiling waitress ushered her to the secluded table he had chosen and handed her a large menu. 'Coffee?' she invited, and when Kelly nodded gratefully, brought a large mug and filled it. Kelly added cream from the jug Joss handed her, refused sugar, and drank deeply.

'That's good,' she said at last. 'I didn't realise how much I needed it! I could drink pints.'

'No reason why you shouldn't,' he told her, looking faintly amused. 'She'll come along and fill you up in a minute.'

'Really?'

He nodded. 'As many times as you like. I know you English always find that a gas—Mark told me. Now, what're you going to eat?'

Kelly opened her mouth to say 'nothing', then caught his eye. Maybe it would be wise to have something, she thought, remembering his threat that he wouldn't be stopping again. But surely he was wrong in saying there wasn't much food in the camp. Mark would be seeing to that—he'd never let her arrive without having made preparation. She closed her eyes, thinking how wonderful

it would be to be with Mark again, and opened
them to find Joss Varney watching her.

'I guess you'll be suffering from jet-lag,' he
remarked as if it were just one more cross he had
to bear, and she lowered her eyes quickly to the
menu.

It was full of oddly-named dishes, things that
were familiar and others that weren't. For instance, what was a 'short stack'? And whoever ate
pancakes with sausages, even if they were called
'pigs in a blanket'? And 'hash browns'—what on
earth were they?

'You're looking at the breakfast menu,' Joss's
voice observed, sounding amused again, and she
quickly turned the menu over. 'Not that it matters—they serve breakfast all day. I just thought
you might rather have something else.'

'Actually breakfast sounds just right,' Kelly
said, turning the menu back. 'I'll—I'll have a
short stack, with bacon and sausages and an egg,
if that's all right.' Nothing would have made her
ask *his* advice on what to eat.

'Fine by me. I was thinking of having the same.'
He glanced up and gave the order to the waitress,
who gave them both a friendly smile and, as Joss
had predicted, filled their mugs with coffee again,
placing two glasses of iced water on the table as
well. A nice idea, Kelly thought, sipping it. Then
she raised her green eyes to Joss Varney's dark
brown ones and said boldly: 'Well, Mr Varney,
you're not driving now. So you can tell me just
what this is all about, can't you? Or have you got

some other excuse for not telling me the truth?'

Her heart hammered against her ribs as their eyes met, but she kept her gaze steady. Something odd seemed to be happening inside her; a kind of weakening of the stomach muscles, a feeling that her body was no longer entirely her own. Jet-lag and hunger, she told herself firmly, and raised her chin defiantly.

'You don't have to look at me like that,' he said quietly. 'I haven't made away with your Mark and scattered his body in plastic bags all over California, if that's what you're thinking.' She gasped and felt her face flame as she began a hasty denial. 'Okay, okay, you don't have to say it. You've been looking at me like I was Jack the Ripper all the way from the airport. And before I start, let's get one thing straight. We don't go a lot for this mister and miss business over here—it gets in the way. So let's start again, shall we? My name's Joss.'

You know my name perfectly well, Kelly thought rebelliously, but she nodded and said: 'All right—Joss. And I'm Kelly.'

But it seemed he couldn't keep things friendly for more than a moment. His lip curled and he said: 'Kelly. What sort of a name is that for a girl? Sounds more like some wild Irishman.'

'It's the name my parents gave me,' she returned coldly. 'And as it happens, my grandfather *was* a wild Irishman—and I'm proud of it!'

His eyes widened a little. 'Is that so? Well, you should be a popular girl over here, then—the

Americans really go for Ireland. But maybe the influence has been diluted somewhat by now.'

Kelly was silent as the meal arrived, then she gazed at it in surprise. A 'short stack' turned out to be a pile of pancakes, flanked by sausages, bacon and egg. Toast and a portion of jam— referred to on the menu as jelly—arrived separately, and there was a jug of brown syrup, which Joss picked up and poured generously over his plate.

Kelly watched in fascination.

'What is it?'

'Maple syrup. Never had it?' She shook her head, opening her mouth to say she didn't want it now either, but before she could speak he had poured an equally generous dollop on her own food. 'Only way to eat it,' he remarked cheerfully, and attacked his own meal without further ado.

Tentatively, seething with anger at his highhandedness, Kelly picked at her food, and found to her surprise that it was good. She suddenly realised how hungry she was and ate ravenously, enjoying the unfamiliar combination of flavours washed down with an alternation of coffee and iced water, until at last she laid her knife and fork down on the empty plate and sat back with a sigh.

Joss Varney was watching her, his dark eyes enigmatic. She found that he had ordered a fruit salad for them both, and as she drew hers to her and began to eat, he said abruptly: 'Right, now we'll talk. You want to know about Mark.'

'Yes, of course I do,' she retorted, her heart quickening. 'What—what's happened to him? Why didn't he come to the airport?'

He shrugged. 'Not a lot to tell. We were working early this morning—wanted to get as much done as we could before you arrived.' *And spoilt everything*, Kelly supplied silently. 'Mark didn't have his mind on the job, I guess. He slipped and crocked up his ankle, that's all. Meant he couldn't drive or anything, so I had to come in for you. That's about all there is to it.'

'That's *all*?' She stared at him. 'So why couldn't you tell me before? Why make such a mystery of it? And just what did Mark do to his ankle? Is it serious? Has he had any medical attention? Is he on his own? And just what is it you're doing anyway, Mr Varney? I never really got a proper idea from Mark's letters.' She leant across the table, her fruit salad, delicious though it was, forgotten. 'Because do you know what I think? I think there's a lot more to this than meets the eye. Mark had a good job in Seattle with that civil engineering firm. He was doing well, getting valuable experience. Then you come along—an adventurer, out for a—a quick nickel, is that the right expression?—and before I know what's going on he's thrown up his job and gone off to California with you on some wild-goose chase that'll end up in him losing all his money and all the opportunities that were open to him before. And now you tell me he hurt his ankle because

he didn't have his mind on his job! What kind
of an excuse is that, Mr Varney? Just what are
you up to?'

There was a long silence. Kelly clenched her
hands together, aware suddenly of interested
glances from other people in the restaurant. The
man in front of her sat perfectly still, only the
faint flush on his tanned cheeks betraying that he
was in the least affected by her angry tirade. His
dark eyes had narrowed slightly, his mouth
thinned to a hard, angry line, and his knuckles
showed white. Kelly knew a moment of pure
fear; adventurer he might be, but she was
suddenly sure that not many people dared to
speak to him in that way, and those who did
would get short shrift from this strangely
powerful man.

But he'd met his match as if he thought he was
going to bully and dominate *her*, she thought,
unconsciously squaring her shoulders and lifting
her chin. Her eyes, green and sparkling as the sea,
met his and for a moment there was an answering
flicker deep in the hard brown stare. Then it disappeared as he sat back and surveyed her through
lazily-lowered lashes.

'Well, you've asked a lot of questions there,
Kelly,' he drawled, though she could detect an
edge of anger in his casual tones. 'And that's why
I didn't tell you about Mark's accident before. I
told you, I don't like chattering women while I
drive! As for your other questions—yes, Mark's
being looked after and I don't think even you

would want to quarrel with the attention he's getting. Not the medical attention anyway. . . . I'm not answering the rest. For one thing, I think you're damned impertinent and don't warrant answering at all. For another, you'll see everything you need to see and know everything you need to know in a few hours, and I don't believe in wasting words. Nor do I believe in explaining myself and my actions to spoilt little girls who'd be a lot better off at home eating boiled eggs and soldiers in the nursery! And now, if you've finished, we'll be on our way. I told you, I want to make camp before dark if possible—though at the present rate of progress it doesn't seem likely we'll make it this side of midnight!'

He stood up abruptly and made his way to the till, while Kelly sat smouldering with rage at his words and his casual dismissal of her. Spoilt little girl indeed! What did he think she was? She was Mark's *fiancée*—she had a right to know what had happened, a right to ask as many questions as she wanted. *He* certainly had no right at all to treat her like this, and when she finally reached Mark and told him how his so-called partner had behaved towards her, she had no doubt that the 'partnership' would be broken up straight away and Mark get back to the good job he'd had in Seattle.

That was if it wasn't too late—if this—this adventurer, this con-man hadn't already wrecked her fiancé's chances. Well, he wasn't going to con *her*. She knew exactly the kind of man he was, and she didn't intend to leave him in any doubt about that!

She got up and followed him to the door, determined to have it out with him before she agreed to go a yard further, but before she could speak he jerked his thumb and said abruptly: 'The rest-room's through there. I'll see you back in the truck.'

As he shouldered his way through the door, Kelly hesitated. She wanted to refuse what had amounted to the kind of command that would have been issued to a small girl; then she reluctantly acknowledged that it was only common sense to make use of the facilities, and she turned on her heel with all the dignity she could muster.

A quick wash and a dash of the pink lipstick that matched her shirt did a good deal to restore morale, she decided, looking critically at her reflection as she brushed her short blonde hair. Green eyes looked back at her, tired and faintly bewildered. Arrival in California hadn't been at all as she had expected. What had happened to her dreams?

Her slim shoulders drooped with a momentary depression; then she remembered Joss Varney and raised her chin. Maybe this was just what he was aiming for! He obviously didn't want her here— realised that she saw through him, she thought contemptuously. Maybe he thought he could frighten her off—well, she'd soon show him how wrong he was! Kelly Francis wasn't to be put off so easily. And, head high and shoulders back, she marched out of the restaurant and back to the Chevrolet.

Joss Varney was already in the driving seat and made no comment other than a grunt and a pointed glance at his watch. Kelly settled herself in her own seat, making sure that she sat far enough away from him to risk no chance contact, and stared out of the window as the Chev swung out again into the traffic.

She knew by now that he would refuse to answer any questions about Mark, but was determined not to give in to his demands for complete silence while he drove. So after a while she asked casually: 'How far is it to your camp, Mr Varney? And where will I be staying?'

But Joss Varney evidently meant what he had said. He merely grunted: 'You'll see,' and turned on the headlights. And somehow Kelly found herself unable to argue. They were in open country now; there was little traffic in the growing dusk, and much as she would have liked to watch the scenery, her first glimpses of a Californian spring, tiredness was overwhelming her. Her head nodded forward, jerked back, nodded again. And the third time this happened, Joss Varney glanced at her and said curtly: 'You'll find a sweater just behind you. Put it behind your head and get some sleep.'

It was for his benefit really, she thought, reaching for the sweater. A sleeping woman couldn't disturb him with chatter! But she was grateful for

the soft comfort as she laid her head back; and
from then on she was only dimly aware of the
rumbling of the Chevrolet's engine as they surged
forward through the deepening night and into the
wild hills.

CHAPTER TWO

IT seemed only moments before she was awake again, refreshed but bewildered as she stared around. There was little to see; outside was a black darkness, the sky lit by a myriad stars. There didn't even seem to be any road. The truck was moving slowly, nosing its way along what appeared to be a rough track—or maybe no track at all. As Kelly's eyes became more accustomed to the darkness, she could just make out craggy rocks on the right, close to the truck. To the left, she could see nothing, but she could hear the sound of rushing water.

Wild panic filled her as all her original fears came back. Where was this man taking her? What was he planning to do? What had he done already, with Mark? *Just who—and what—was he?*

'Let me out!' she gasped as sick terror rose in her throat. 'Let me go!' She struggled frantically with the door-handle. 'Stop—please stop!'

Joss Varney reached across and grabbed her arm, his fingers like a vice. 'Stop that, you stupid little fool! You'll have us in the river! My God, don't you have *any* sense?' The Chev stopped abruptly and he crushed her back into the seat, using both hands to pin her down, his body almost covering hers as he forced her to stop struggling.

For a moment they remained motionless, their faces so close that she could feel his breath on her cheek, see the angry glitter in his dark eyes. She was breathing hard, her breasts touching his chest as they heaved, but he made no attempt to move away. Instead, he seemed to ease himself a fraction closer, so that she was intensely aware of his hard body so tauntingly near hers.

Her lips parted and her eyelids closed of their own accord; a strange weakness invaded her body; but even as she acknowledged his strength and power, she felt him twist away from her with a muttered exclamation, and slowly she sat up, rubbing her wrists.

'Now look,' he said brusquely, starting the engine again. 'We're on an old dirt road. It runs right above the river and, as you may have noticed, it's dark, so it takes a bit of concentration. Just keep quiet and keep still, and don't treat me to any more displays of hysterics. I warn you, I shan't take much more!'

He didn't say what he'd do, Kelly thought, crouching as far away from him as she could get, but it wasn't too hard to guess. Ever since she had first seen him at the airport she had been unnervingly aware of his male virility. No doubt he was the sort who thought of women as good for one thing only. Well, thank goodness she'd be with Mark soon. And tomorrow, or as soon as he was fit to move, they would be out of here—away from this mountebank and the influence he seemed to have gained over her fiancé—and away

from the strange and frightening effect he seemed
to be having on her. . . .

She said nothing more as the Chev ground its
way along the rough, bumpy track. Where they
were going, she had no idea; she still didn't know
what the 'camp' was, or what it was for. Only the
thought of seeing Mark kept her from crying out
again as she caught glimpses of the swollen dark
river below, the rocks that strewed their way. But
when at last Joss pulled the truck to a halt on a
small grassy platform by a clump of gnarled trees,
she couldn't repress a gasp of horror.

'Is—is *this* your camp?' she whispered, staring
at the single orange tent illuminated in the head-
lamps and pitched close down beside the water.

'This is it,' he responded cheerfully, swinging
himself down and coming round to open her door.
'And mighty glad I am to see it!'

'But—but it's just a small tent! It can't be where
you and Mark—and where *is* Mark?' she added,
her voice sharp with anxiety when she realised
that the camp was deserted.

'Why, you didn't imagine he'd be here, did
you?' Joss's voice was casual to the point of indifference as he grabbed a rucksack and strode off
down the bank towards the tent. 'I told you, he's
getting good attention. He's in the nearest hospital, being waited on hand and foot by pretty
nurses. You don't have to worry about Mark!'

'But——' She stared wildly around, then ran
down the bank after him. 'But where am *I* to stay
the night? I thought—I thought——'

He stopped and faced her, huge in the starlight. 'You thought I'd take you to some nice luxurious hotel for the night. Well, let me inform you, Kelly Francis, there ain't no such animal in this neck of the woods! You're out in the wilds now, or maybe you hadn't noticed! And don't blame me for that—it was you who insisted on coming. I'm just the poor mug who had to drive two hundred miles to fetch you and two hundred to bring you back. If you think I'm taking you another hundred yards to find somewhere that'll suit you to lay your pretty head, you've another think coming! *This* is where you'll spend the night, *Miss* Francis—in this little tent with me. You can have Mark's sleeping bag, so you'll sleep warm. And you needn't look so appalled—I shan't turn into a werewolf before your very eyes.' He bent and rummaged in the tent, coming out with a hurricane lamp which he lit and handed to her. 'Now, take care with that and don't burn the place down, it's all we've got. Get some of those clothes off, if you want to, and get into that sleeping bag—the red one. I'll be back in five minutes, so make it snappy!'

Kelly watched speechlessly as he strode off into the darkness. Then she turned and looked into the tent. It was bigger than a two-man, but there was so much equipment piled along one side that there was room only for the two sleeping bags to lie side by side, touching. She couldn't sleep there—she *couldn't*! How dare he even ask it of her! She'd wait till he came back, then she'd tell him it was no go. Or—better still—she'd make it a *fait accompli*.

Rapidly, Kelly crawled into the the tent and slipped out of her slacks and shirt. Clad only in lacy bra and pants, she slithered into the red sleeping bag, then quickly rolled up the blue one and thrust it outside.

That would show Joss Varney that he didn't give all the orders round here!

It seemed only second before she heard the quick, firm footsteps as Joss came back down the bank. Something dropped with a clatter close to the tent; there was a muffled exclamation and then a clear oath. The door of the tent shook and was ripped open as Joss glared in.

'What the hell's all this about?' he demanded, holding up the sleeping-bag. 'What's this doing outside?'

'It's for you to sleep in.' Kelly tried desperately to keep the quaver from her voice. He mustn't guess she was scared of him! 'I'm not accustomed to sharing a tent with a strange man.'

'Oh, you're not, are you?' His voice was grim. 'Well, here's a chance for you to start getting accustomed to it! Because you're not throwing me out of my own tent, young Kelly, don't you think it! I'm coming right in there with you, and if you don't like it that's just too bad!'

'Oh, no, it isn't!' Kelly sat up, forgetting the scantiness of her attire as the sleeping bag fell away from her. 'Look, I didn't ask to be brought here! I didn't even come to see *you*, hard though you might find that to believe. I came to see Mark—my fiancé—and when he knows how you've treated me——'

'Mark! *Your fiancé!*' Joss's tone was withering. 'Why, he's just a kid—the pair of you, you're both kids! You don't know what you're talking about, either of you—love, marriage, all that scene's for adults, grown-up people, not children, don't you realise that? Look at the way you've tied him down, before he's had a chance to see anything, before he's had a chance to learn what it's all about! And you can't even leave him alone when he does start—you've got to come chasing half over the world to see what he's up to, to make sure he doesn't get his feet wet or get in with bad company. Why can't you slacken off the apron strings—let him go, let him learn to be a man? And at the same time, maybe you could learn to be a woman!'

His eyes went to her breasts, almost fully revealed in the flimsy bra, and Kelly felt herself blush scarlet as she hastily pulled the sleeping-bag up to cover herself. She was horribly aware of how vulnerable a position she was in, half naked in a tent with this terrifying man, miles from anywhere.

'My relationship with Mark is nothing to do with you,' she said coldly. 'As soon as I can, I shall be seeing him—and make no mistake, he's going to hear all about the way you've treated me. And I don't know what it is you're doing here, camped on this river-bank, but whatever it is it

can't be all that important. And whatever it is you
hope to get out of Mark, I'm afraid you're going
to be disappointed—because I'm going to do my
utmost to see that he goes straight back to Seattle
to get his old job back, if it's not too late. And
now—I'm tired. I want to go to sleep.' She thrust
back the blue sleeping-bag which he had pushed
into the tent again. 'Take that, and go and sleep
in your precious truck!'

Joss stared at her, his bulk seeming to fill the
doorway of the tent, and she stared back, more
scared than she would admit even to herself, her
heart hammering as his eyes narrowed and his face
paled with anger under the tan. The atmosphere
in the tent was electric; the slightest movement
would cause an explosion, she thought as she held
her breath, disturbingly aware that the pounding
of her blood matched the wild roar of the river
close outside. Then Joss Varney moved. There
was no explosion—but one might have been pre-
ferable, she thought, as she shrank away from his
invasion of the tent.

'Quit talking and move over!' His hands
gripped her body, lifting her easily, sleeping-bag
and all, to one side. 'I've had just about all I can
take of you and your acting up.' He laid the blue
sleeping-bag out flat while she watched, trembling, knowing that further protest would be use-
less. Then he quickly unbuttoned his shirt and
ripped it off, revealing the tanned, hairy chest she
had known must exist under the blue denim.
Next, his hands went to the waistband of his jeans,

and she couldn't hold back a tiny squeak of dismay as he peeled them from his long muscular legs and stood clad only in a pair of brief blue pants.

'Well, *now* what's the matter?' he demanded. 'Don't tell me you've never seen a guy get undressed before? Or maybe you're one of these girls who only like it in the dark—though I didn't think there were many of that kind left these days!'

'It just depends what kind you're used to mixing with, doesn't it!' she flared. 'It may surprise you to know, Mr Varney, that there are still a few of us who *don't* jump into bed with every man we happen to meet. Still a few of us who like to wait for—for——' She floundered to a halt, disconcerted by the mockery in his eyes.

'For the right man to come along?' he finished for her sarcastically. 'Well, well, who'd have believed it? So young Mark's got through to you where no other man's managed it, has he? He's a better man than I took him for after all! No wonder he damn near broke his leg with the excitement of seeing you again!'

'Don't talk like that!' she snapped, raising herself on one elbow. 'Mark's a better man than you'll ever be, Joss Varney! And not because of what you think! Because *he* doesn't think women are just for one thing only—he doesn't try to force his fiancée to do anything she doesn't want to do, he loves my mind, not just my body, he——' Again she stopped. The look on Joss's face, dawning incredulity combined with something else, something she couldn't and didn't want to recognise, drove all the words from her mind—drove everything from her mind, leaving her aware only of the sensations of her body, unfamiliar, frightening, yet strangely exhilarating. . . .

'Do you mean to tell me,' he began wonderingly, 'that you and Mark have never—that you're a *virgin*?' She nodded helplessly, mesmerised by his eyes as a rabbit is mesmerised by a stoat, and he gave a short laugh. 'My God! Poor Mark! And you've been engaged for—how long?' She opened her mouth, but he silenced her. 'And you say he doesn't try to force you to do anything you don't want to? My God, my foolish, foolish little virgin, don't you think that if you really loved him, if you were really adult enough to love each other as adults do, you *would* want to?' He stared at her, taking in the elfin face with the green eyes under the tumble of blonde hair, his eyes moving down to the breasts that were once more revealed in their lacy covering. 'Do you even know, you poor innocent, what it feels like to want to love a man—to want *him* to love *you*?'

He was nearer now, as near as he'd been in the truck. Kelly wanted to move, to cry out, but her limbs seemed to have been paralysed, her voice reduced to a husky whisper. She stared at him, wide-eyed, as he came closer still and she felt the heat of his body on her bare flesh. His arms came round her, drawing her to him, pressing her against his naked chest. Strong hands caressed her back as she began to struggle, but her struggles seemed to have no more effect on him than those of an imprisoned butterfly and, as she began to plead, to beg him to let her go, his lips silenced hers with a kiss; tender at first, so that after her first gasp she was aware only of an invading sweetness that parted her own lips, a weakness that left her limp in his arms. Then the kiss deepened, bruised her mouth, and the passion in it called for an equal response from her. Of their own accord, it seemed, her arms found strength, crept up round his neck, her fingers moved in his dark hair and she arched herself towards him, moaning a little, moving her body against his, revelling in the feel of his hairy chest against her own soft skin. His lips left hers, moved down to her throat, his teeth nipped gently at her shoulders; and then, as his hand slipped round from her back and cupped her breast, he raised his head and looked down at her.

'So I was right,' he said softly. 'You *don't* know—or you didn't! Hell's teeth, isn't there anyone in charge of you, you pretty little innocent? Don't you have a nursemaid to look after you?'

She stared up at him, aware that her face was flushed, her hair dishevelled, her arms still linked behind his neck. Then she gasped and drew back, recoiling as if from a snake. Shame washed over her as she pulled the sleeping-bag up around her shoulders and spat her words at him.

'No, I don't! And I shouldn't think she'd be

much good if I had—I'd need an army to look after me while you're around!' Contempt darkened the green eyes as she glared up at him. 'It's easy to see what kind of a man *you* are— trying to seduce your partner's fiancée while he's injured in hospital. Well, you're a big, brave man, Mr Varney, and there's no one around to hear me scream—why don't you go ahead? Why don't you prove to us both what a man you really are? Only don't expect me not to make my mark on you— I've been growing my nails especially!'

There was silence as she finished, broken only by the noise of rushing water outside and the thundering of her heart within. She tensed her body, half afraid of the reaction she might provoke, ready to defend herself. But Joss Varney, after a long moment during which he seemed as tense as she was, did nothing. He merely turned away with a short laugh and said: 'Don't tempt me! I told you before, I'm not a cradle-snatcher.' Then he slid into his own sleeping-bag and turned out the hurricane lamp.

'That was just a lesson,' he told her in the darkness. 'Don't imagine it was anything else. Now let's get some sleep!'

Kelly lay rigid, aware that if she allowed herself to relax she couldn't help her body touching his, and even through the thickness of two sleeping-bags the thought of the contact repelled her. She would never sleep tonight! Instead, trying to take her mind off the man who lay so close to her, she began to think back over the day, the extra-long day that had resulted from flying with the sun.

So much seemed to have happened since she left London that morning. And nothing had turned out as she had expected. By now, she should have seen Mark, talked with him, sorted out all the things that had puzzled her in his letters. By now, she might even have persuaded him to give up this crazy scheme, whatever it was, and return to Seattle. But instead. . . .

Her thoughts returned inevitably to the man who lay breathing gently beside her; the man who had taken her roughly in his arms and kissed her with a strange tender passion, waking sensations she had never known before, calling for a new and violent response which her body had made eagerly even while her mind repudiated it. Shame at her unexpected behaviour, coupled with humiliation, burned her like a fever. What would Mark say if he knew? Well, he *would* know—at least, he'd know of Joss Varney's treatment of her. Make no mistake about that.

It was daylight when Kelly was next aware of anything. She woke slowly, opening her eyes in bewilderment to the soft orange glow of the sun through the walls of the tent. The sleeping-bag was warm and cosy, and during the night she had curled herself up in it. It was several moments before she realised that round her was curled the body of Joss Varney.

She froze. She could feel the contours of his body plainly against her own. She had her back to him and lay with her legs crooked; his, crooked in the same way, fitted neatly to her, as if she were sitting in his lap. Worse still, the two bags had slipped down in the night; his naked chest pressed closely against her back, and his arm lay heavily across her waist.

She had to get out of here—she *had* to! The memory of last night flooded her mind. He hadn't gone any further then—but what would he do when he woke and found her virtually in his arms? Kelly had no illusions about Joss Varney's virility. He was the sort of man who needed women, contemptuous though he might be for their worth for anything other than sex. And he had already demonstrated his scorn of her engagement to Mark—*that* wouldn't stop him from taking what he wanted.

He seemed to be sleeping heavily and Kelly began, very slowly, to squirm out of the sleeping-bag. Space was restricted and she was unable to move without touching him. Thank goodness he didn't seem to be waking! She wriggled a little more, then unzipped the bag so that she could escape more easily. Her heart was thudding as she felt the length of him, almost naked, against her. His arm still lay across her body, imprisoning her; she tried to lift it, couldn't, and began to panic, squirming against him in her increasingly frantic efforts to escape. The sensation of skin against skin made her head swim, and her breathing quickened as she felt his hand tighten on her stomach and realised that he was awake.

'Let me go!' she panted furiously, trying ineffectually to pull his hand away. 'Let me *go*! I want to get out!'

'Are you sure of that?' he drawled in her ear, and she felt his lips against her neck. 'Y'know what? I thought I was just having a lovely dream—and then I woke up and found it all coming true!' For a moment, he held her against him so that she could feel the hardness of his body. 'And y'know something else—for a virgin, little Kelly Francis, you sure know how to wake a man up in the morning!' He let her go so suddenly that her body fell away from his, then with one quick movement he grabbed her and twisted her round on to her back. He raised himself above her and stared down into her face. 'I think it's time we got up now, don't you, Cat's Eyes?' he said with a quietness that frightened her. 'The sooner I can get you out of here and back with your *fiancé*, the better!'

Kelly lay trembling as he grabbed his shirt and jeans and left the tent. Outside she could still hear the endless cascading of the water; nearer at hand was the sound of birdsong. The tent was filled with the flow of sunlight filtering through the orange canvas. The air that came in through the open flap was fresh, cool and invigorating.

Slowly she sat up and found her slacks and shirt. She would have liked to put on fresh clothes—these felt as if she had been wearing them for ever—but she knew that it was no use asking Joss Varney to bring one of her cases down from the truck. However, she was determined to change before going to see Mark.

There was no sign of Joss as she stepped from the tent and slowly stretched her arms above her head. She looked around her with delight. In any other circumstances she would have thought this a truly idyllic spot. The tent was pitched on a grassy bank, close to the edge of the water. Above it, the low cliff was tufted with shrubs and flowers. Pink blossom grew close to her head, and she reached out and touched it wonderingly.

The river itself was about thirty feet wide and at this point it swept round a wide bend; a few yards downstream the water broke white and wild over a series of smooth rocks. On the far side the rock rose sheer out of the water in a smooth grey cliff, and she realised that up here she was among mountains.

A slight sound made her turn quickly and she saw Joss coming along the bank towards her. He was wearing only a towel knotted round his waist and had obviously been in the water; drops glistened among the hairs on his chest and made rivulets down his long legs. He shook back his wet hair and reached for his denims which lay across a rock.

'You can go and get washed if you like,' he told her abruptly. 'There's another towel here—it's Mark's, you needn't be afraid to use it!' he added mockingly. 'And I'd advise you to get going fast, if you don't want your maidenly susceptibilities to be even more upset—I'm going to strip off now!'

Kelly grabbed the towel and fled. She had no doubt that he would do just what he threatened if she stayed! Nothing embarrassed that man, she decided, wandering along the river bank until she came to a small, sheltered pool in a hollowed-out part of the bank. Well, so long as he didn't come along here she ought to be safe. And with a quick glance round her, she slipped out of her clothes and into the water.

It was icy! Gasping with shock, she scrambled for the bank. She'd never know water so cold! Why hadn't he warned her? She pulled the towel round her and rubbed herself, shuddering violently as she did so. Her body positively ached with the cold—but as she towelled, she began to feel a tingle, and a few minutes later, clad once more in slacks and shirt, she felt warmer and certainly wide awake. But she was still shivering a little as she made her way back to the camp.

Joss glanced up as she approached. He had a small camping stove going and she held out her hands, hoping for warmth. He reached behind him into the tent.

'Here, put this on.' He tossed her a thick, warm sweater and she pulled it gratefully over her head. 'Bit of a shock, was it?'

His mocking smile angered her and she retorted: 'You could have told me it was so cold! Why is it, anyway?'

'Should've thought you'd know that. Look around you. Look *up*. Up there.' Kelly followed his pointing finger uncertainly. 'Well? What d'you see?'

'Mountains,' she said. 'Mountains and—oh! Snow.'

'That's it. Snow. It's snow melting that's making the river run so fast and so cold. And it's snow melting that brought me here. Me and Mark.'

'I don't understand,' she said, accepting the mug of coffee he handed her and curling her fingers round it.

'No, I don't suppose you do. And I know Mark didn't tell you—had some fool idea he'd keep it as a surprise for you. I knew it'd cause trouble!' He slapped ham into a frying-pan and put it on the stove. 'Look, you're in California, right? Up in the hills, by a river. There's a lot of water coming down because it's spring. Doesn't that tell you anything?' And when she still gazed blankly at him he sighed with exasperation and said: 'Look around you. Look at the equipment.'

Kelly stared around. Beyond the tent, half hidden by shrubs, was an assortment of strange-looking equipment—something that looked almost like a large vacuum-cleaner, an iron platform, a peculiar arrangement of—sieves? A sluice? She looked back at Joss and shook her head.

'I don't know,' she said. 'What *are* you doing?'

'My God,' he muttered, 'haven't you ever heard of *gold*?'

'*Gold?*'

'Yes, gold. Did you think it was just an old-fashioned story? *Tales of the Motherlode* and all that? Didn't you realise it was still there, to be got? Well, that's what we're doing. Getting gold. And that's why you're such a nuisance, wishing yourself on us just as we're getting some results, and landing my partner in hospital!'

Kelly stared at him. She scarcely heard his last words as the meaning in what he had told her sank into her mind. *Gold!* So that was why Mark had been so secretive—that's why he'd thrown up everything, jettisoned all their plans to come away with this man! No wonder he hadn't told her what it was all about. He knew her well enough to be able to predict her reaction.

'You mean you brought Mark here to look for *gold*?' she gasped. 'You persuaded him to leave the good job he had—the opportunities—to come on some wild-goose chase after gold? Do you realise what we were going to do? We were going to get married! Mark was going to find us a house and I was going to come to Seattle. We'd been planning it for years—yes, years. Oh, you may think us very young and childish, Mr Varney— after all, you must be all of thirty yourself—but Mark and I grew up together. We've always known we'd get married some day. And when Mark decided to emigrate, we agreed it would be better for him to come over first and get settled. That's not childish and irresponsible, is it? I stayed at home, and I just lived for his letters. And then, when he was doing so well in his job with the civil engineering firm in Seattle, we decided to make it a Christmas wedding. He was

coming home for it—we were going to come back
together——' She broke off suddenly and buried
her face in her hands. 'And now you've spoilt it
all! You've lost Mark his job—you've put all kinds
of crazy ideas into his head—and nothing will be
the same again, ever! I hope you're proud of
yourself, Joss Varney, I really do!'

She raised her head. Joss Varney was cooking
breakfast, as if he hadn't heard a word she'd said.
He lifted the ham out on to a plate and held it out
to her. Furious, she slapped his hand aside and
the plate flew out of it and landed upside down.
There was a sizzling as the ham touched the dew-
wet grass and, before Kelly could stop it, slithered
down the bank and into the water.

'Pity,' said Joss, sliding the rest of the ham on
to another plate and beginning to eat. 'You're
going to wish you hadn't done that before the
morning's out.'

CHAPTER THREE

By mid-morning Kelly was forced to acknowledge that he was right. They were on their way to Mawani, the small town where Mark was in hospital. Since breakfast, they had said little. Kelly had gone to the truck and taken some fresh clothes from her case; she was now wearing a pale blue suede skirt and jacket, with a white sweater that emphasised her small, rounded breasts. She had listened without comment as Joss Varney had shown her the gold-dredging equipment, explaining how either he or Mark, wearing a wetsuit, would dive to the bottom of the river to shift large rocks and manoeuvre the hose, which then sucked debris—including, they hoped, gold—to the surface to be sluiced. It was hard work, he said, and though the rewards could be large they were certainly earned.

She had even managed to say nothing when he told her how Mark's accident had happened. They had got up early, it seemed, in order to get some work done before Mark had to leave for San Francisco to meet her. Joss wasn't sure even now just what had gone wrong—but Mark, wearing the wetsuit, had got himself caught in the rocks. By the time Joss had realised he was in trouble, he had injured his foot and half drowned. Joss had got him out, done what he could for him, then taken him to Mawani before heading straight for San Francisco.

'So you don't know how he is now?' Kelly had asked then, her green eyes wide with horror. 'You just left him there—and didn't bother even to ring up? Why didn't you tell me? I could have gone last night——'

'You couldn't!' Joss turned on her angrily. 'I told you, he was getting good attention. There was nothing more I could do—I never reckoned on having to go all the way to San Francisco to meet you, as it was! Would you rather I hadn't bothered—left you there, wondering, while I stayed in Mawani and held Mark's hand?'

'No, but——' Kelly floundered, then recovered herself. 'You could have taken me there last night, instead of bringing me here!'

'I couldn't. Look, you know how late it was when we got here. It'd have taken us another hour to get to Mawani. They wouldn't have let you in at the hospital at that hour—and you wouldn't have found anywhere to stay, either. I checked in the morning. There's a rodeo on there all this week and the place is ram-jam full.'

Kelly was silent. She didn't know whether to believe Joss or not—all she did know was that, whatever he did, it would be what suited him best, and however much she argued, he would always have the last word.

Well, it wasn't for much longer, she told herself as they came into the little town of Mawani. Just as soon as she could get Mark away from here, they'd be saying a last goodbye to Joss Varney. And, so far as she was concerned, it couldn't be a moment too soon!

The restaurant they passed on the edge of the town reminded her of her missed breakfast. But there was no time to think of that now; the Chev was rumbling down the main street, past wooden buildings and verandahs—there was even a horse tied loosely to a rail outside the small branch of the Wells Fargo bank. Kelly recognised a vague feeling she had had ever since arriving in America—that she had somehow strayed into a film and was one of the stars. She half expected to see Clint Eastwood come striding from the saloon.

Her thoughts were interrupted by the Chev turning to the left, into the hospital grounds. She stared at the building, suddenly uneasy.

'You go on in,' Joss said abruptly as she climbed down. 'I've got to go to the bank. I'll be along later.'

Kelly watched him go; then, with an odd feeling of foreboding, she turned and went into the hospital.

It was larger than she had expected for such a small town; presumably it served a large country area as well, she mused as she enquired for Mark at the desk and was handed over to a young and pretty nurse. As she was led through the corridors, Kelly was conscious of the girl's curious glances, and her feeling of uneasiness grew.

Exasperated, she told herself not to be silly—it was all the fault of that Joss Varney, upsetting her. It was Mark she was going to see now—Mark, the boy she had grown up with, the boy she had always planned to marry. Mark, who never humiliated her or stirred her senses and left her with that indefinable ache somewhere inside . . .

The nurse opened a door and Kelly went in, her face stiff.

'Hi. Long time no see.' Mark was sitting up in bed in a small room on his own. He was grinning, but there was something vaguely defensive in his smile, and Kelly approached his bed with some hesitation.

'Mark. What have you been doing to yourself?'

Hardly a passionate greeting, she thought ruefully as she bent to kiss him. And that was hardly a passionate kiss. But what was she thinking of? She had never looked for passion from Mark, only gentle, affectionate love. And if the sample she had received from Joss Varney was passion, she didn't want it anyway, thank you very much. She was perfectly happy with what she'd got.

'Guess I was just a bit careless,' said Mark. 'It was the excitement of you coming, I expect—that's what Joss reckoned, anyway. Sorry—means I won't be able to show you around. I'll be in here for a few days yet, I'm afraid.'

'Oh, Mark! How bad is it?'

'Nothing too serious,' he reassured her. 'They

just think it's best for me to be here, for X-rays and things. Seems I've broken some small bones in my foot. And there's nowhere else to go anyway, the town's full. Where did you stay the night?'

Now was her chance—her chance to tell Mark just how Joss had behaved towards her, to incite his anger at her humiliation. But now that the moment had come, Kelly found she didn't want to any more. She didn't understand why and didn't much want to analyse her feelings—at least, not right now. She only knew that whatever had passed between her and Joss, she wasn't going to tell Mark after all.

'Oh, Joss looked after me,' she said vaguely, and Mark's face cleared.

'I knew he would. He's a great guy, isn't he? I've never met anyone quite like him before.'

'Nor have I,' Kelly said feelingly. 'Mark, why did you come here? Why did you throw up everything to chase after gold? It's crazy, can't you see that? You had a good job—good prospects. Why give all that up to spend a few weeks endangering your life in that freezing river looking for something you might never find? And why didn't you tell me what you were doing? Why keep it all so secret?'

Mark's face changed. He looked sullen and turned away from her.

'Because I knew this was how you'd react, that's why. Because you'd try to stop me, and I *wanted* to do this, Kelly, don't you understand?

Because—because if you must know, I'm fed up with you running my life!'

Kelly stared at him, unable to believe her ears. Could this be Mark—her gentle, affectionate Mark, always so ready to listen to her suggestions, so eager to please her? She shook her head in bewilderment—and then she knew the reasons for the change.

'It's Joss Varney, isn't it?' she demanded. 'He's been getting at you—oh yes, he's said the same things to me, more or less. Chaining you down before you've had a chance to live. Keeping you tied to my apron strings. But you know that isn't true, Mark. We're a partnership—you were working for *us*. Don't I have a right to a say in what happens?'

Mark turned restlessly in the bed. Kelly watched him anxiously, remembering her feelings of foreboding and realising at last that it was this that had brought her all the way from England—a subtle change in Mark that had come through to her in his letters, telling her that all was not well, even though there was nothing she could put her finger on. The feeling must have been growing in her for weeks—months—almost without her knowing it, a subconscious fear that even now she could not fully explain.

'Mark,' she said quietly, 'what is it? Something's happened, hasn't it? You've changed. Tell me, Mark. If nothing else, surely I have a right to know *that*.'

There was a long silence. Mark was staring at

the blankets, picking at them with his fingers, clearly uncomfortable. At last, without meeting her eyes, he spoke.

'Yes, you do have that right, Kelly. It's just— well, I don't know quite how to say it. Maybe it would've been better if I'd written to you—told you the truth. But by the time I'd realised what was happening—well, you'd bought your ticket. And there didn't seem any point in telling you then. And I thought perhaps, when I saw you, I might feel differently. . . .'

His voice faded away. Kelly sat in the chair, feeling as if she'd been turned to stone. It wasn't hard now to see what he was getting at, and it was so totally unexpected, so much beyond any of her indefinite misgivings, that the shock left her feeling drained and breathless. She waited for Mark to say more, but he had evidently run out of words, and at last she found her own voice.

'Are you telling me you don't want us to be engaged any more?' she asked quietly, and Mark looked almost grateful.

'Yes—yes, I suppose I am, really.' He gave her a half shy, half apologetic smile. 'I know it must seem an awful shock to you, Kelly, after all we'd planned. But Joss is right, you know—we did get engaged rather young and neither of us has had much chance to see anything of life. It's not just me, Kelly,' he went on earnestly. 'It's not fair on you, either. I mean, you were as tied down as I was. Girls do all sorts of things nowadays—travel, have careers and all that. I don't want you to miss anything.'

'That's—that's very thoughtful of you.' Kelly kept her temper, though her heart was beating fast. To come all this way just to hand back a ring! And Mark didn't seem to have any real idea of what he might be doing to her. As she looked at him, it struck her for the first time how very young he actually was. She was two years younger than he, but suddenly she felt years older. Maybe she had grown up in their months apart; maybe it was the contrast between him and the experienced Joss Varney. But it seemed to her now that they must have been slowly moving towards this point for a long time—and now that they had reached it, it was almost a relief.

'Well, you'd better have this back.' She slipped the tiny diamond ring from her finger and held it out, shaking her head firmly when he tried to refuse it. 'What will you do now? When you get out of here, I mean. You won't be able to go back to the camp, will you?'

Mark's face was rueful. 'Not really, Joss needs someone who's really fit to help him. No, I guess I'll just have to high-tail it back to Seattle.'

'Seattle? To your old job? But will you be able to get it back again?'

He stared at her. 'Get it back? I never lost it. It's there for me at any time.'

'But you threw it up,' she protested. 'You threw it up to come on this—this crazy chase for gold.

How can you be so sure they'll be keeping it open for you?'

'Kelly, don't you realise?' Mark exclaimed, as if she ought to have known all along. 'It's not like that at all. Joss Varney's not just a gold-dredger. He's my *boss*—my boss in Seattle. He owns the whole set-up—and a lot more besides. He owns firms in Alaska and California, as well as Washington. Joss Varney's a big man out here, Kelly. Do you mean to say that you didn't know that?'

The main street of Mawani was quiet, its wooden shiplap houses and shops set against a background of tree-clad hills, with the mountains of the Sierra in the distance. Kelly wandered aimlessly, pausing to look in the assortment of shops—funny, old-fashioned places that sold knitting-wool, books, groceries and gardening tools in a cheerful miscellany. In the tiny hardware store she found saucepans, cowboys' hats and gold-panning equipment ranged side by side along the shelves. There was a small art gallery and a museum, where she stared at some of the machinery once used for mining gold, and saw how the history of the area had developed since the Ahwahnee Indians were first driven from the Yosemite in the early days of the gold rush; when San Francisco Bay had been a truly golden gate for those sailing round the Horn from the eastern states to delve for the new riches. Yosemite was now a National Park, its beauty preserved for the enjoyment of those who loved the wilderness. In the tiny tourist information office, Kelly gazed at postcards and maps, showing both Yosemite and the King's Canyon Park which would still, the man behind the counter told her, be deep in snow.

'It's very picturesque up there,' he said, opening a book to show Kelly pictures of the giant sequoia trees that were such a feature of King's Canyon. 'They clear the roads just as far as the Snow Lodge Motel—people go there for the skiing, and a lot of folk have cabins there too. It's real pretty. Not that Yosemite isn't as well, that's spectacular with its mountains and waterfalls. But it gets mighty crowded in the summer.'

Kelly thanked him and went on her way armed with a sheaf of leaflets and cards. Well, it seemed that there were worse places to come to get jilted, she thought wryly. And with six weeks to go before she could return to England, she might as well enjoy herself. Fortunately, she was able to afford it; Mark had offered to help her if she needed money, but she had taken some pleasure in tartly reminding him that now they weren't getting married she was free to use her own savings. She had already arranged with her own bank at home to draw funds from the Bank of California, so there was no problem there.

The question was, just what to do next? Mawani, picturesque though it was and close to the wilderness she longed to explore, didn't seem to be the best place to use as a jumping-off point if you were without transport. There was no railway and Kelly had so far seen no sign of any bus service. Presumably everyone here had cars. She might be able to hire one—though even that might present difficulties, since she would probably then have to return the car to Mawani at the end of the hire period.

The best thing would probably be to go back to San Francisco and hire a car there. She could then come out again to visit the National Parks, and see something of the city as well. Meanwhile, there was a more pressing problem—that of food. It was now past lunchtime and Kelly had been for some time regretting her lost breakfast. She stood irresolute for a while, then remembered the restaurant she and Joss had passed on the way into town and set off towards it, blessing the American way of life that kept restaurants open all day, and sometimes all night, for those who didn't eat at the conventional times.

She was halfway through her meal, the leaflets spread on the table in front of her, when a shadow fell over her.

'So this is where you are,' Joss Varney said harshly. 'I've been looking all over for you.'

'I don't know why you should do that,' Kelly retorted. 'We made no arrangements to meet again. You can go back to your gold and forget all about me now.'

He sat down opposite her and ordered his meal quickly, with only a glance at the menu.

'I just happen to have your luggage in my

truck,' he said sarcastically. 'Or don't you want it any more?'

Kelly was silent. She had forgotten her luggage, and cursed herself inwardly for her foolishness. It seemed that whenever Joss Varney was with her, he was able to catch her out in some way.

'Well, you can just take it out now you've found me,' she said. 'I can look after it from now on.'

'Can you?' His dark eyes met hers, the thick brows raised. 'Mind telling me just what you plan to do?'

'Yes, I do mind,' she retorted. 'I don't see that it's any business of yours now.'

He didn't reply to that but began to eat his meal. Kelly picked at her own. Her appetite seemed to have gone. Just what *was* she going to do? She would have to decide soon—there was nowhere to stay in Mawani, she had checked that for herself. And she wasn't going to ask this over-bearing brute for help—no way! She knew just what kind of help *he'd* be likely to give—another night in the tent, and if he found out that she wasn't engaged to Mark any more, any inhibitions he might have had on that score would be immediately removed.

Her stomach twisted at the thought of what might happen during another night in the tent with Joss Varney—but it wasn't going to happen. And she wasn't going to tell him about Mark, either. That was certain.

As it happened, she realised a moment later,

there was no need to tell him anyway. The dark
eyes met hers again and he said abruptly: 'You're
not wearing your ring.'

Kelly cursed his observation. She might have
known nothing could be hidden from that probing
gaze. She shrugged and said levelly: 'No. Mark
and I decided—we decided to call it a day.'

It didn't seem to come as any surprise to him.
He nodded and chewed his food thoughtfully.
'You don't seem exactly brokenhearted.'

'I don't wave my feelings about for everyone to
see!' she snapped.

'No? I hadn't got that impression at all,' he
drawled, and she felt her face flame as she recalled
the way she had responded to the intimacy of the
kiss he had given her last night.

'Well, I suppose you're pleased about it,
anyway,' she said sulkily. 'After all, with all your
great experience you never did think I was the
right girl for Mark, did you?'

Joss finished his coffee before replying, and
Kelly watched him, simmering. How could he be
so maddeningly calm and indifferent about it?
After all, it was largely *his* fault that Mark had
got these crazy ideas into his head. And he might
be a 'big man' in three of the States, but that
didn't mean *she* had to be impressed by him!

'No, I didn't think you were right for Mark,'
Joss answered eventually. 'I didn't think he was
right for you, either, and I thought it even less
when I met you yesterday. You're well out of it,
Kelly. Count your blessings—and start to live.'

'Thanks!' she scowled. 'When I need your advice, I'll ask for it. And now, if you'd kindly let me have my luggage I'll get out of your way and you can go back to your *gold*.' She put as much contempt as she could into the last word. She couldn't understand why a man like Joss Varney—wealthy, the owner of the countless civil engineering and mining concerns, as Mark had told her—should desert it all for three months every year to camp out on a riverbank and virtually live rough while dredging for gold. It had seemed quite natural when she had thought him an adventurer, making money where and when he could, even though she had been angry that Mark should ally himself with such a man. But now that she knew the truth . . .

'He needs to do it,' Mark had told her. 'It's a kind of holiday to him—like other men go mountaineering, or sailing.' But Kelly still believed there was more to it than that. Joss Varney wasn't the man to do something just for kicks. There had to be some bigger reason.

The lust for gold, she told herself. She had caught something of the atmosphere of the old gold-rush days during her visit to the museum. The fever still lingered on in many men, and Joss Varney was one of them. He wasn't satisfied to make money through his various companies. He had to dig the raw gold from the earth, gloat over it as the old forty-niners had—and probably spend it as fast as they did too. Well, he was welcome to it. Kelly had seen for herself what sudden wealth did to people, and she wanted no part of it.

'And just what are you going to do when you've got your luggage?' Joss asked mildly. 'Hitch a lift back to 'Frisco?'

Kelly felt her face flush. He knew, of course, that there was no transport. 'I'll think of something,' she muttered. 'You don't have to worry about me, anyway.'

'Unfortunately, I do,' he retorted. 'God knows why—but I feel responsible for you, Cat's Eyes. And don't think I wouldn't rather just get up from this table, turf your cases out of the truck and drive off into the sunset—there's nothing I'd like better. But——' he shrugged '——I just don't seem able to do that. I know you came here because of Mark, and I brought Mark here in the first place. Moreover, I may be partly responsible for his change of mind——'

'I don't doubt you are!' she flared at him. She ran a hand through her blonde hair and her green eyes flashed danger as she went on, 'You've done nothing but poison his mind against me ever since you met him, I can bet on that. Telling him we were too young—telling him I was tying him down—I wonder what else you told him? And why? You want to know what I think, Mr Varney?' She paused, but he said nothing and his dark eyes were veiled. 'I think you've had one hell of a big jilt yourself some time! Someone's really knocked that oversized ego of yours and given it a bruise you've never got over. And that's why you can't bear to see anyone else happy—because you just don't know how to be happy yourself!'

She stopped, breathing as hard as if she'd been running, her white sweater heaving. Joss Varney sat perfectly still. His jaw was tight and a muscle twitched in his cheek. Well, at least he can't do anything to me *here*, Kelly thought, putting her hands down on her lap so that he shouldn't see them shaking. And I'll take good care he doesn't get me alone anywhere!

'I think we'll pretend you didn't say that,' Joss said at last, speaking very quietly, and she knew that she had touched and angered him more deeply than ever before. 'What I was going to say was that as I was partly responsible for bringing you here, I feel I should at least get you somewhere where you can find a place to stay and get yourself organised for the rest of your time here. When do you go back to England?'

Not soon enough for you, Kelly thought. Aloud, she said: 'In six weeks. I have to stick to that date—it was a condition of the advance purchase ticket I bought.'

He nodded. 'Well, that's time to see quite a bit. But you ought to rest up a bit for the first few days. You're bound to have jet-lag—and it hasn't been exactly restful so far, has it?'

There might almost have been a spark of humour in his voice then, but Kelly was determined not to acknowledge it. She said stiffly: 'You really don't have to worry, Mr Varney. I can look after myself.'

'I thought we'd agreed it was Joss?' Startled,

she let her eyes meet his. She was momentarily shaken by the unfamiliar look in them, then it was quickly veiled and coldness took its place. 'Look, let's quit beating about the bush. I know somewhere you can stay for a few days, and you can fix your own transport then and head off where you like.' His glance fell on the leaflet, open at a picture of the Snow Lodge Motel. 'You could do a lot worse than that, too. It's quite a place.' He waved away the waitress's offer of more coffee and stood up. 'Let's get going.'

Kelly stood irresolute. She badly wanted to tell this arrogant man to stop arranging—and dis-arranging—her life. But if she refused his offer—and after all, it *was* only the offer of a lift—what else was she to do? It was getting late in the after-noon and she had nowhere to stay, no chance of finding anywhere in Mawani, and no way of get-ting to another town. She didn't even know how far it was to the next one!

Once again, it seemed, Joss Varney had the upper hand. And if she had disliked him before, she loathed him now—if for no other reason than that he always seemed to get the last word! But it seemed that there was nothing else she could do.

'All right,' she said, comforting herself with the thought that once he had delivered her at this place, wherever and whatever it was, she need never see him again. 'But I think I'll just visit the rest-room first, if you don't mind waiting.'

That, at least, was one order she'd managed to forestall!

CHAPTER FOUR

BACK in the Chevrolet Kelly gave herself up to thought. So much had happened to her since her arrival in California, and all of it unexpected. Mark's changed attitude, coming so soon after the ordeal of her night with Joss Varney, seemed to have left her numb. Cautiously, she explored her feelings. Surely she should be feeling more upset than this? Joss had said she didn't seem brokenhearted, and she had to admit the truth of his remark. Piqued, disillusioned, a little sad for the passing of the happy times she and Mark had shared—but not brokenhearted.

Her main emotion was still anger with the man who, she believed, had deliberately brought this situation about. For some reason best known to himself, Joss Varney had wanted Mark's engagement to end. He had encouraged feelings of dissatisfaction, a restlessness that she would have sworn was alien to Mark's character. And yet how much did she really know of the boy she had grown up with? She would have sworn, too, that he would never behave as he had towards her today. Had she been wrong all along the line? Maybe it was a mistake to trust any man, she thought as the Chev rumbled along the country road, between rolling hills and wide green

pastures. She had thought Mark the most stead-
fast of men and she had been mistaken. So who
could she trust? Better not to trust any.

Glancing at her watch, she realised with surprise that they had been travelling for over an
hour, and she turned to Joss, forgetting his in-
junctions not to talk, and asked urgently: 'Where
is it you're taking me? How much farther is it?'

'I'm taking you to a house of mine.' Joss never
took his eyes from the road as he made his brief
reply. 'It's near Carmel.'

'A house of *yours*?' she gasped, hearing her
voice squeak with horror. 'But I never thought—
there's no need, really—just drop me at a motel
somewhere, that's all you need do!'

'You have to be joking.' He slowed down for a
bend. 'Drop you at some motel in the middle of
nowhere? You'd be better off back at the camp.
Now, quit arguing. I'm taking you to my place
and that's all there is to it! You'll be quite safe,'
he added sardonically. 'I've got a Scottish couple
looking after it, very straitlaced. There'll be no
sharing a sleeping-bag at Pacific Glade.'

'Pacific Glade?' A suspicion formed in Kelly's
mind. 'Where did you say this house was?
Carmel? Where's that?'

'Right next to Monterey, Cat's Eyes,' he
answered laconically. 'Down on the beautiful
Pacific seaboard, a hundred and fifty miles south
of San Francisco.' There was a note of amusement
in his voice as he mocked the tones of a holiday
courier, but Kelly was in no mood for laughing.

The Pacific seaboard! Why, that was miles away! It would take at least three hours to get there. Of course, it was obvious what Joss Varney was up to. He wanted to get her as far away from Mawani as possible—away from any possible reconciliation with Mark, she thought furiously. But how dared he? How dared he pretend he was taking her just a few miles and then whisk her half across the State? As if she were a parcel to be picked up and put down just wherever it suited him.

True, poring over maps before she had left England, she had picked on Monterey as one of the places she would like to visit, and had read John Steinbeck's *Cannery Row* specially, in preparation. But she would have liked to make her *own* choice as to when she went there and where she stayed. Not be virtually kidnapped by a man whose arrogance and sheer, inflexible high-handedness left her breathless; a man who had more or less admitted to deliberately wrecking her engagement, who had forced her to share a tent with him; who had kissed her the way Mark had never done, and touched her body with fingers of fire. . . .

She couldn't go to stay at his house, she *couldn't*! Even if there was a whole Scots clan looking after it. Yet what could she do about it? She couldn't jump out of the Chev while it was driving steadily along these roads. And even if she did escape, where could she go? There were few houses in this quiet countryside; just a farm here and there, with a few buildings dotted around it. And it wouldn't be long before it began to get dark again. Moreover, there was the problem of her luggage.

'Look, I'm not going to hurt you,' Joss said impatiently. 'You don't have to sit there biting your nails and trying to think up ways to get away.' Kelly flushed scarlet; the man could even read her mind! 'And you needn't think I'm doing this just for your benefit. I've got to go down to Carmel anyway. I can't do any more dredging till I get a new helper—I've got a guy coming down from Alaska, but he can't get here for several days. So I'm going to use the time looking at some of my other concerns around the state. I use Pacific Glade as a base. I won't even be there, most of the time!'

That was a relief, anyway. But she wouldn't stay there a moment longer than necessary, Kelly made up her mind about that. All right, there was nothing she could do about it tonight—but at the earliest possible moment she was going to make her own arrangements. And she wouldn't be asking for Joss Varney's approval!

'Did you say you were getting someone to come down from Alaska?' she asked after a while. It was all very well for him to say no talking, but you couldn't travel in silence the whole way.

But Joss seemed a little more inclined to be sociable than he had yesterday; maybe because today he hadn't had to deal with getting an injured man out of a river and into hospital, plus a round trip to San Francisco, Kelly thought ruefully. He

nodded and said: 'A cousin—works at the original
family mine up there. That's where I hail from,
you know, Alaska. My great-grandfather went to
the Yukon, made his pile, founded the family
fortunes. Since then, we've expanded; gone into
oil and civil engineering as well as gold. I ran it
with my father till he died a year back. It keeps
me busy most of the time.'

But not too busy to go gold-dredging, she
thought. The old fever still burned in the blood.
And it burned hot enough to destroy any care he
might have had for others—Mark, for instance. It
hadn't worried him that Mark, unused to the
work, might endanger his life. It hadn't bothered
him that he might be breaking her heart when he
persuaded her fiancé to break their engagement.
And for what reason? She whipped her anger up
again. Just for his own personal satisfaction, that
was why. Just because at some time—she was sure
she was right about this—someone had hurt his
male pride, bruised his ego. Well, good for her,
whoever she was. Kelly congratulated her. It must
have taken some doing.

They reached Carmel just as darkness was falling, leaving the freeway for Ocean Street and
driving down the quiet, tree-shaded road past ex-
pensive-looking bungalows to the main part of the
little town. Kelly gave a soft 'Oh' of delight as
they came into the main street. There were no
lamp-posts, just lanterns glowing in the trees. By
the soft light from the shop-windows she could
see displays of glass, sculpture and pictures. It

was totally unlike the other towns and cities they had passed through on their way. Here were no rows of motels and restaurants with their flashy signs and hoardings; here were no neon signs or glittering fairy lights to catch the attention. The streets were quiet, even the traffic seemed more discreet, and the whole place was imbued with an air of elegance and good taste.

'They practically have a public meeting if someone wants to erect a dog-kennel here,' Joss remarked, threading his way through the streets. 'And you sound your horn at your peril! But everyone likes it. It's got something nowhere else has got, and there's a lot of people want to make sure it stays that way.'

'Oh, I hope it does.' Kelly leaned forward eagerly to see through the windscreen. 'I liked Mawani too—but this is beautiful.'

Joss gave her a quick glance. 'Funny, I'd have thought Mawani would bore you stiff.'

'No! It was fascinating—and it was real, too. I mean, real people lived there. It wasn't just for tourists. It wasn't full of souvenir shops.'

'And of course, you're not a tourist,' he mocked her. 'You're different. Aren't they all!'

Kelly flushed and bit her lip. Once or twice during their drive this had happened—she had felt, almost against her will, a kind of rapport growing between her and this brusque man. And each time, as soon as it appeared, he had slapped it down, deliberately keeping the distance between them, it seemed.

They were out of the little town now and heading for the coast. In a few minutes they were on the beach road and Kelly was gasping again as she looked out over silvery sand-dunes across the Pacific Ocean. Its rolling blue waves, crested with glittering white foam, merged with the dusk of night, while the glow of sunset branded a path of fiery orange from horizon to shore, and a few early stars pricked the deepening purple of the sky like sparkling needle-points.

The road climbed high along the cliffs and the sea lay below, now crashing at the foot of sheer crags, now breaking more gently on sandy coves. Joss swung the Chev off the road and down a rough track. Kelly noticed a wide gateway, shrubs, and trees that reared high into the sky. Then they were twisting down to a long, low house set halfway down the cliff. The truck stopped and he turned off the engine.

The sound of Pacific rollers crashing on rocks far below could now be heard as a muffled roar. Somewhere close at hand, a bird called. Kelly climbed stiffly down and stood with the soft breeze lifting her hair, dazed, weary and unable quite to take in where she was. With the cessation of engine noise and movement, fatigue overtook her and she swayed, putting a hand out blindly to save herself.

'Here,' Joss said roughly in her ear, 'you're just about all in.' And she felt two strong arms lift her, swinging her through the air. Thoroughly exhausted now, she wanted to protest, but could only murmur as she turned her head. She looked up into the shadowed eyes and time seemed to pause as their glances locked. Her heart and blood seemed stilled; even the crashing of the waves faded. Through his shirt, she could feel Joss's heart beating strongly against her cheek. She tried to remind herself that she hated him, that he had done his best to wreck her life. But somehow she couldn't repress a sensation of having come home; of having found the place she was meant to be. . . .

'So you've arrived, Mr Joss!' The voice startled them both, and Kelly jerked in Joss's arms as he turned quickly towards the house. A stout, elderly woman stood there, her hands folded in front of her, her face as serene and unsurprised as if Joss were in the habit of bringing girls home every night. As he might well be, Kelly thought, wishing he would put her down but knowing it was of no use to struggle. This must be the Scots housekeeper—there had been a faint tinge of brogue in the voice. At least he had been telling her the truth about that.

'I've made your rooms ready,' the woman went on. 'My, the poor child looks worn out! Get her inside, Mr Joss—Andra can see to the luggage. I've made some good broth for you both and I'll have it on the table in no time.'

The weariness that had overtaken Kelly so abruptly on the previous evening seemed to have struck her again. Jet-lag, she thought bemusedly as Joss carried her indoors and dumped her un-

ceremoniously on a large, fur-covered sofa. She
lay against the cushions, trying to summon up the
energy to move to a more dignified position, but
could scarcely keep her eyes open. Then the
Scotswoman appeared with a steaming cup and
she struggled up to a sitting position.

'A good cup of tea for you,' the housekeeper
declared, setting it on a small table. 'I'll warrant
that's what you've been missing. They dinna
know how to make it here at all—d'you know, they
give you a cup of hot water and a tea-bag if you
ask for it in a restaurant! Coffee, yes, they
understand that—but for tea, they're hopeless.'

Kelly laughed and drank the tea while the
housekeeper watched benevolently. 'That's right!
That'll wake you up a bit—long enough to take
some broth, anyway. My name's Shona, by the
way, and my husband's Andra. We live at the back
of the house, so we'll no be disturbing you.'

And just what did she mean by that? Kelly
wondered ruefully. It looked as if Joss was indeed
accustomed to bringing girls home and not wanting to be disturbed. Well, the sooner she made it
clear that they weren't on those terms, the better.
. . . Not that it mattered. She wouldn't be staying.

She looked around the large room, taking in
the details that made it so different from an
English living-room. The decor—the strange furniture, apparently made with huge slabs of wood
and covered with fur so that it looked almost
primitive, yet sensual, setting an atmosphere of

virile masculinity that suited Joss Varney right
down to the ground. There were some good
pictures on the walls too—a pictures of violent
seas and raw cliffs, of remote mountains and
tangled forests. The kind of pictures a tough,
active man would like. And at the far end of the
room—where a huge picture window looked out
over the ceaselessly-moving Pacific—surely that
was a small swimming-pool! Forgetting her
weariness, Kelly walked over to it and stood staring, bemused, at the blue water that lapped Italian
ceramic tiles. With all the Pacific outside—and
there was another pool, a large one, just beyond
the terrace—who would want a miniature swimming-pool in the lounge?

'It's a hot tub,' an amused voice said from the
door. 'A whirlpool—a jacuzzi. Haven't you ever
come across one before?' Joss came over to her
and stood close.

Kelly shook her head and he laughed; a low,
mocking, sensual laugh. 'We'll have to introduce
you to its delights, then. It's like an underwater
massage when you switch it on.' His hand touched
her shoulder, then moved down her back, caressing her gently with slow spiralling motions, while
Kelly stood frozen beside him, unable to move or
speak, possessed suddenly of an intolerable longing to turn towards him, to rest her cheek once
against against that hard chest, feel the strong
beating of the heart, the warmth and power of his
body against hers. . . . 'It's for company bathing,
you understand,' he went on, and his voice was

soft, purring. 'Not half as enjoyable alone.'

His fingers were lightly touching her side, moving up almost to her breast, then back to her hip. The ache that was now becoming familiar to Kelly was spreading over her body. Stop it, she wanted to scream, stop it—I don't even *like* you! But he didn't stop; he went on, letting his finger-tips roam casually over her body—and Kelly didn't know whether it was a relief or a disappointment when Shona's voice called that their supper was ready and Joss let his hand fall away from her. She only knew that Mark had never made her feel like this—that she didn't want to feel like it now—and she wished passionately that neither of them had ever come to California. That neither of them had ever set eyes on Joss Varney.

The smell of freshly-made coffee, mingled with the perfume of blossom and the tang of the sea, was the first thing Kelly was aware of when she woke next morning. For a moment she lay still in the large, comfortable bed, revelling in the feel of cool, smooth sheets against her skin. Her eyes moved slowly round the room, taking in its sparse yet luxurious furnishings and huge window over-looking the Pacific. Then a sound brought her attention to the door and she sat up as Shona came in, carrying a tray.

'Oh, you shouldn't have done that!' Kelly exclaimed, looking with pleasure at the tray and its contents of steaming coffee-pot, orange juice, fruit and covered plate. 'I could easily have come downstairs.'

'Mr Joss gave orders that you were to have a good rest.' The Scottish housekeeper's accent was an oddly attractive blend of her native dialect and American. 'He says you've had a wearying time of it.'

True, but Kelly was surprised that Joss Varney should have bothered to take it into account. She lifted the cover from the plate and looked with appreciation at the scrambled eggs and thin slices of ham with tomato. Shona watched approvingly as she began to eat.

'I like to see a healthy appetite,' she observed. 'Some of these young girls today eat nothing at all. They look like sticks, and no wonder! Mind, you're no' so very fat yourself, Miss Francis. You look as though you could do with a bit of feeding up.'

'It doesn't seem to make any difference,' Kelly confessed, pouring herself some coffee. 'Mmm . . . heaven! And what a beautiful view. It's a lovely spot—have you lived here long?'

'Over twenty years. Andra's brother was over here and kept badgering us to come out, so we did—just for a visit, but we liked it and stayed. We've been with the family all that time—we used to work for old Mr Varney, then when he died and Mr Joss built this place he asked us to come here. We wouldn't want to leave it now.'

'So you've known Mr Varney—Joss—for a long time.' Kelly finished her eggs and ham, and peeled a banana.

'Aye, since he was a wee lad.' The older

woman's face softened. 'And he hasn't changed—
just got worse, I tell him! You know him well
yourself, Miss Francis?'

'No, we only met a couple of days ago,' said
Kelly, wondering if that could possibly be true.
Joss Varney seemed to have been a prominent
feature in her life for months now! And not a very
welcome one, either. 'He really needn't have
brought me here at all—and I can't stay. I'll have
to start looking for somewhere else as soon as I
can. D'you know of anywhere round here, Shona?
Somewhere not too expensive.'

The housekeeper stared at her. 'But you'll not
be going just yet! Mr Joss said you'd be staying a
few days at least. You need to rest, he said.
There's no question of you finding somewhere
else, not for a while anyway.'

'But there is,' Kelly argued, trying to decide
whether to feel amused or annoyed at this
assumption that she would do Joss Varney's
bidding. 'There's no reason at all why Mr Varney
should put me up here. He hardly knows me. Oh,
I appreciate it, of course—but now that I've had
a good night's sleep and a breakfast I couldn't
possibly impose on him any more.' Why not tell
her the truth? a small voice inside her asked. Tell
her you've just *got* to get away—because the effect
Joss Varney has on you is something that scares
you stiff and makes you want to run a thousand
miles. Tell her that your stomach twists when you
think of the way his hand moved on your body
yesterday evening, or the feel of his skin against

yours when you woke in the tent. Tell her the feel of his kiss is burned into your memory like fire— and that you've got to escape from him before worse happens.

But she knew she wouldn't tell the friendly Scotswoman any of this. And when Shona, lifting the tray away from her, repeated: 'It was his orders that you have a good rest, Miss Francis. He *wants* you to stay'—Kelly could only look at her and ask helplessly: 'And does Mr Joss always get what he wants?'

Shona stood by the bed, balancing the tray on her hip, and answered thoughtfully, 'Mostly he does, yes. In fact, I can't call to mind any par-ticular time when he hasn't. Except—except——' And her face shadowed suddenly.

'Except for when?' Kelly asked curiously.

'Oh, it was a long time ago. Something went badly wrong for him, you see. Something—well, I've never really known all the ins and outs of it. But he's never really got over it, never been quite the same. It—well, I suppose you could say it embittered him.' She sighed.

Kelly watched her. She was dying to ask more questions. So she'd been right—something *had* made Joss Varney the overbearing cynic he was today. And she wouldn't mind betting she was right about what it had been, too.

'Was it—was it a woman?' she asked, aware that Shona was unlikely to tell her the whole story, but needing to know that.

'Aye, you could say that. Though whether

woman would be the right term, I'm not so sure.'
The older woman's eyes met Kelly's and they
were bright with tears. 'Still a bit of a girl she was
when it all happened. Cassie, they called her.
They'd not been married long, not long at all. It
was a great shame.'

'*Married?*' Kelly repeated in astonishment.
'You mean she was his wife?'

'Aye, that's what I said.' Shona took Kelly's
empty coffee-cup and set it on the tray, indicating
quite clearly that she was saying no more. 'Well,
I must be away back to my kitchen. I've lunch to
prepare, and it's time I was started. Now, you're
to go wherever you like around the house and
garden, Mr Joss says, but don't wander too far,
will you. You're still looking a bit peaky to me,
and I think he's right to make you stay here and
rest for a few days. You'll find me in the kitchen
if there's anything you need.'

Kelly watched as the door closed, then lay back
against the pillows. So Joss Varney had been
married! And maybe still was—though something
Shona had said seemed to imply that the marriage
was over. Well, it was probably just as she'd
thought—Cassie, whoever she was, had decided it
was a mistake and left him. And Shona, who had
known Joss since boyhood and evidently doted on
him, naturally thought it was a tragedy.

Well, perhaps it was as far as Joss was concerned, Kelly thought, staring idly from the
window at the blue, rolling sea. It had certainly
given his ego one almighty whack. But as for

Cassie—wherever she was now, she was probably a good deal happier than she could ever be married to Joss Varney. It was no tragedy as far as *she* was concerned!

Kelly stretched luxuriously and slipped out of bed to wander to the window. The sea, azure under the morning sun, was beating at a reef some little way from the foot of the cliff; inside the reef was a small cove, almost a lagoon, where the water lay tranquil, lapping gently on white sand—perfect for bathing. But between this and the house were the cliffs—hanging gardens would be a better word, she thought, staring down at the luxuriant foliage, the brilliant-coloured blossom and carpet of ice-plants that covered every inch of ground. Immediately below her window was a wide terrace, with chairs and a comfortable-looking swing seat dispersed around it. At one end was the swimming-pool, for use when the sea was too rough for bathing, she supposed, and on the remainder of the wide shelf on which the house was built grew a mass of plants and trees, some known to Kelly, others exotically unfamiliar.

It really was a paradise, she thought, regretting that she must leave. But there was no question of that. There was no reason for her to stay here, no reason for Joss Varney to continue to feel responsible for her. It was probably to do with this idea he had that anyone under twenty-five was an infant and therefore incapable of looking after themselves. Well, she'd have to disabuse him of that idea. And as for his wanting her to stay—

well, Shona had certainly got *that* wrong! Not that it would have made a scrap of difference if he had. . . .

Kelly went into the bathroom attached to her room and showered, thankful to be able to wash her hair which had suffered from the flight followed by the night in the tent. Feeling rather more human, she found her suitcases, intending to pick out some fresh clothes.

They were empty! Bewildered, she stared at them and then around the room. She went over to the built-in wardrobes and slid open the doors—and yes, there were her clothes, all neatly hung up. Her underwear was arranged tidily in the drawers.

Shona must have done it while she was asleep, Kelly thought. Well, it was a bit much! Oh, she didn't blame the housekeeper—she'd been acting under instructions and probably thought Kelly intended to stay—but by what right did Joss Varney take over her life like this? He knew she wanted to move on.

And what was his purpose anyway? He didn't like her any more than she liked him. Though perhaps *liking* didn't come into it as far as he was concerned—the kind of man he was probably wouldn't bother about that. To him, she was just an unattached woman; a body; a sex object.

'And that's just where you're mistaken, Joss Varney!' Kelly muttered to herself, slipping on a dress of watery green that matched her eyes. 'So you've got a reputation for always getting what you want—well, this is where you find how wrong you are!' And she left her room, head high, determined to find him and have it out with him at once.

But the house appeared to be empty. There were sounds coming from the kitchen, but doubtless this was Shona, preparing lunch. It seemed unlikely that Joss Varney would be helping her! Kelly wandered through the house, opening doors, peering into rooms that each spoke equally of their owner's wealth, taste and uncompromising masculinity. A smaller sitting-room with a large fireplace and comfortable furniture. A study, the desk spread with papers and maps, the walls hung with more maps and old mining prints. A games room, large enough to run a youth club in. And finally, the spacious living-room she had seen the night before, with its fur-covered chairs and sofas, and its jacuzzi blue and inviting by the enormous window.

The window was, she discovered, made up of several sliding glass doors. Beyond it lay the terrace; and, stepping through, she discovered at last Joss Varney, lying back in a sunlounger and reading a newspaper.

CHAPTER FIVE

'Oh!' Kelly exclaimed, taken aback.

Joss tossed his newspaper aside and studied her mockingly. His appearance was totally different today and Kelly stared speechlessly at him, her green eyes taking in the cream slacks, the dark brown silk shirt that exactly matched his eyes and hair, the gold Rolex Oyster watch on his wrist. Everything about him spelt money; he could have been a different man from the rough gold-dredger, driving a battered Chevrolet truck, who had forced her to spend the night in a small tent high up in the mountains. . . .

'Seen enough?' he enquired sardonically, and Kelly's face grew warm. Shrugging, she turned aside and looked out over the sea.

'You must admit it's quite a transformation,' she observed coolly. 'You look quite respectable now.'

'Respectable!' He have a short laugh. 'I never dreamed I'd hear you call me *that*! I thought you looked on me as the original answer to every maiden's nightmare.'

'Not every maiden's, perhaps,' she countered, and saw his face darken. 'As it happens, I was looking for you. I need to talk to you. I think Shona has the wrong idea about my stay here.'

'Really?' he murmured, and Kelly flushed again at the wicked glint in his eyes.

'Yes,' she went on determinedly. 'She seems to think I'm spending some days here. I tried to tell her I'd be leaving at once, but she didn't seem to understand. . . . She's unpacked all my things. I don't want to hurt her feelings, she's been so kind, but maybe you could tell her the true position.'

'And that is?'

He was looking at her with a disturbing, penetrating glance. As if, Kelly thought, he was trying to will her to make some specific answer. . . . She turned her back on the ocean and clutched tightly at the rail behind her, answering lightly: 'Why, that I'll be leaving this afternoon. I expect you know of somewhere I can stay—somewhere simple—and a place I can hire a car. Then I can be on my way and you can forget all about me. You really don't have any responsibility towards me, you know. You've done quite enough already.'

'That's a matter of opinion!' In one movement, he was on his feet and, before Kelly could move had her pinioned against the rail, a hand on each side of her, his arms like steel bars from which there was no escape. She was terrifyingly aware of his body close to hers. His shirt, unbuttoned almost to the waist, revealed the dark hairs on his chest and she saw the glint of gold from a chain he wore round his neck. Her breathing quickened, but she was determined not to respond in any way, and she stood rigidly in the circle of his arms.

'Look at me!' His hand grasped her chin, forcing her to meet his eyes again, and she saw that
they were as hard as polished stone. 'Now, what's
all this about leaving? I told you you were to stay
for a few days.'

'Oh, yes, so you did!' Trembling, she tried
nevertheless to match his sarcasm with her own.
'Those *were* your orders, weren't they? But it just
so happens, Mr Varney, that I don't want to obey
them—I don't *have* to obey them. I'm not one of
your employees—or maybe you'd forgotten that.
Maybe you're such a big tycoon you think everyone's an employee of yours! Well, some of us are
still free, does that come as a big surprise? And
some of us intend to stay free. You can't order me
about, Joss Varney! You brought me here against
my will, but you're not going to keep me. I said
I'd leave this afternoon because I didn't want to
hurt Shona's feelings over lunch—well, now I've
changed my mind. I want to leave now—and *you*
can explain to her why!'

'You do, do you? And just how do you propose
to do that?'

Kelly twisted helplessly, but she couldn't shift
the arms that held her against the rail. Behind her
there was a drop of fifteen feet or more to a rock-
ery—no escape there. Defeated, she looked up at
him again.

'Please let me go,' she whispered, feeling tears
come to her eyes. 'Please—why do you want to
keep me here? What do you want of me? You
didn't know me until two days ago. You don't

even pretend to like me. Why do you want to make me stay?'

He stared down at her and something seemed to change in his eyes. Kelly felt her blood freeze as he took one hand from the rail and lifted it to her cheek. Slowly, he ran his fingers from ear to shoulder; then encircled the slim column of her neck. Helpless to prevent him, she stood still as his other hand moved to the centre of her back and he held her against him, so that she could feel the length of his hard body against her own. He lifted her face to his and lowered his lips until they met hers, parting them demandingly.

Kelly quivered in his arms. She wanted to protest, to cry out, to wrench herself from his embrace. But something else rose inside her, something that pushed her thoughts aside and made feelings, sensation, the most important things. Reason took second place as she gave herself up to his kiss, scarcely aware that her own arms had crept up round his neck, that she was arching her body against his, responding to his passion with her own fiery ardour. His hand left her face and crept down to her breast, and Kelly gasped as his fingers found the tautness of her nipple. As his lips left hers to burn a trail down her neck, she hung back across his arm, her head filled with the crashing of the waves far below, her body a surging cauldron of emotion such as she had never known before.

'And you ask why I want you to stay,' he murmured at last, lifting himself away from her and looking down at her with triumph in his eyes. 'Don't you see, little Kelly—you're ripe for a few lessons. And I'm the one to teach you!'

To her astonishment, he pulled away from her then, took her by the shoulders and tossed her into a sun-chair as if she were a doll. She gazed up at him, her eyes dark, her hair tousled, still painfully aware of the clamour of her body. Slowly she passed a hand across her forehead; realised that the front of her dress was half open, her bra pulled away from her breast, and hastily gathered them together. Joss Varney watched, an ironic smile twisting his lips, and from her confusion she felt the familiar hate surge within her.

'What do you mean?' she muttered. 'I don't understand.'

'No, I know you don't. That's just what I aim to change. As you are now, you're a danger to any man who comes near you, Kelly Francis. Most of all, you're a danger to yourself. And I'm not letting you leave here until you *do* understand.' He dropped back into his lounger. 'You tell me you're a virgin—O.K., I believe you, though I didn't at first. Not till we'd spent that first night together. And it was just about then that I started feeling responsible for you, remember? Hell's teeth, did you really think I *wanted* to come chasing halfway across the State to get you to a safe place? But once I realised you'd broken with Mark and were aiming to head off on your own——'

'I can look after myself!' Kelly interrupted heatedly. 'I'm not a child.'

'No, and that's just the point,' Joss retorted. 'You're very much a woman, and I don't think you even realise it. There's not many about like you these days—and a damn good thing too. Because you know something? Your particular brand of proud innocence, combined with your looks and body and the fire you've got inside, could be just calculated to drive men mad! O.K.——' he held up a huge brown hand as Kelly began to protest again—'I know you don't mean it that way. But that's the way it *is*. And until you know how to cope with yourself and the reactions you set up, you're just not safe to be let loose.'

'And you see yourself as my teacher, do you?' Kelly sneered. 'I can guess just what you mean to teach me, too.'

He sighed. 'Quit being so suspicious, little Cat's Eyes. Look, if you want to stay a virgin, you stay one. It's your privilege and I don't aim to take that from you.' *Not much*, Kelly thought. 'But you're underestimating your own nature,' he went on. 'There's a whole lot of fire in you that's only waiting for one match to set it ablaze. Without your engagement to hold you back, you could be easy prey for any unscrupulous male who happens to come along——'

'Like you!' she flashed. 'And I suppose you think all this—this *celibacy* was terribly unfair on Mark. A kind of refined torture, is that it? Well for your information, Mark never tried to force me to—to go to bed with him. So maybe you're overestimating this fire you talk about. All men aren't like you, you know!'

'Wouldn't be too sure about that,' Joss Varney replied thoughtfully. 'Oh, Mark's a nice guy, he respected you. But that doesn't mean he didn't suffer from the same urges any man'd feel. And when he got out here, saw other guys having fun, living as men ought to live—well, it was nothing short of torment. Why else should he have broken loose as he did——' He stopped abruptly. Kelly sat very still, feeling suddenly numb. For once, Joss Varney seemed at a loss to know what to say. He turned aside, fumbling in his pockets for something he didn't seem able to find.

'Well, go on,' Kelly said at last, her voice barely above a whisper. 'Finish what you were saying. About Mark—breaking loose.'

'It doesn't matter,' he said shortly. 'It was nothing important.'

'Go on,' she insisted quietly. 'I want to know. I've a right to know.'

'Look, it won't help——' he began, then stopped. His eyes rested on her, noting her pale face and burning green eyes, the way her dress revealed the curve of her soft young breasts. 'Well, maybe it will at that,' he went on slowly. 'Maybe it'll make you see. . . .' He thought for a moment, then said quietly: 'Mark never meant to do anything but play fair with you, Kelly, I'm sure of that. But he came out to the States never having known any girl but you. As I understand it, you started going out together while you were

still at school, that right?' Kelly nodded. 'And
Mark didn't go away to college, he went to one
near your home town to do his training in civil
engineering. So you were able to keep on seeing
each other—and he never got the chance to make
other girl-friends.'

'He never wanted it,' she said indignantly.
'Neither of us did. We knew we were in love—we
knew we wanted to get married. And if he hadn't
met you——'

'You would have got married, I know. And
maybe you'd have been happy—at first. But then,
sooner or later, it's my bet you'd have made each
other as miserable as hell——'

'You can't know that!'

'I said it was a bet—and a pretty safe one, too.
Look, I've seen what happens when kids get
married too young. They don't know what it's all
about! They've never given themselves a chance,
never got to know anyone else, never learned the
difference between puppy-love and the real thing.
O.K., sometimes it works out; more often, it
doesn't. I didn't want to see that happen to
Mark—I guess I'd gotten kind of fond of him. I
took him about, introduced him to a few girls—
and he began to see what I was driving at.'

Kelly was on her feet, her eyes blazing. 'You
did that! You deliberately encouraged him to play
the field—to be unfaithful to me! How dare you—
how can you sit there and tell me——'

Joss Varney looked calmly up at her. 'He was
never unfaithful to you, Kelly. From what you've

both told me, there was nothing to be unfaithful
about——'

'We were *engaged*!'

'And he'd never even kissed you. Not the way
I've kissed you—had he? Admit it, Kelly—there
wasn't anything between you and Mark, not
really. No real passion. And how far do you think
your marriage would have gone without it? Look,
I've saved you from years of unhappiness. Can't
you see?'

'No, I can't,' she flashed at him. 'All I can see
is that you're obsessed with sex! That's not
everything in a marriage, or maybe you didn't
know that. Love isn't just sex—it's tenderness and
affection and trust, those are the important
things!'

'And do you actually believe,' he asked quietly,
'that if those had really been there, Mark would
have behaved the way he did? Broken out—dated
a different girl each night—let you think everything was all right—got himself in such a state
over it all that he forgot what he was doing the
other morning and half killed himself in the
river?'

Kelly stared at him, then flung herself back into
the chair and began to weep. 'It was your fault—
yours!' she cried through her tears. 'You led him
astray—he was upset and guilty—we *would* have
been happy, if only you hadn't interfered!'

'So why aren't *you* brokenhearted?' he persisted
ruthlessly. 'Because you're not crying for a lost
love, you know—you never did. This is just

temper because someone's taken away your favourite toy—your status symbol.'

Kelly stopped crying. She felt for a handkerchief and wiped her eyes. Then she sat up and faced Joss Varney.

'You seem to know it all, don't you?' she taunted him, her voice shaking. 'And no doubt you know it all from experience. After all, you've known what an unhappy marriage was like, haven't you? You've been jilted yourself—by your own wife, because she couldn't stand living with you any more. And that hurt, didn't it? It hurt so much you can't bear to see anyone else happy. You've got to spoil it for them—you've got to destroy it. *You're* the spoilt baby, crying for a lost toy, not me!' She jumped up, looking down at him as he lay unmoving in the sunlounger. 'Well, you've managed to wreck my engagement—but you needn't think that gives you the power to run the rest of my life. I'm leaving here today, and I hope and pray I never see you or hear about you again. As far as I'm concerned, you're the *dregs*!'

She turned back into the house, but before she could step inside Joss Varney was beside her, his fingers like a vice round her wrist, his other hand tangled in her hair as he twisted her to face him and wrenched her head back, forcing her to meet his eyes. She quailed at the fury that blazed in them, the rage that distorted his ruggedly handsome face, the bitterness that twisted his lips as he said through his teeth: 'And just where did you hear that pretty little story?'

'Let me go! You're *hurting* me—let go of my arm!' Frantically, she struggled, trying to pull away from his grasp, but his fingers only tightened painfully and the tears sprang to her eyes as she felt some of her hairs give way.

'You'll only get hurt the more if you struggle,' he told her savagely, and pulled her closer against him. 'Just answer my question—who's been telling tales? Who's been filling your head with this—this slander? Come on—tell me!'

'I didn't need to be told,' she flung at him, incensed by his brutal treatment of her. 'It was obvious from the start that some woman had got across you at some time! And it's true, isn't it? You did get married?'

'I did, yes,' he admitted with a growl. 'But it wasn't like you think—and I'd still like to know who told you, and what other lies you've been swallowing!'

'I don't think they were lies,' Kelly countered. 'I think it was the absolute truth Shona was telling——'

'*Shona?* You say *Shona* told you? I don't believe it!' He had both her arms now, holding her close to the shoulders, and he began to shake her mercilessly. 'Give me the truth, damn you—who told you? It couldn't have been Shona——'

'But it *was*!' Tears of pain and anger streamed down Kelly's cheeks. 'She told me this morning—told me you'd been married and it—it went wrong. She said it was a great shame, it embittered you—but if you ask me, I think Cassie had a lucky escape, I think——'

'I'm not interested in what you think!' The pure animal savagery in his voice startled her into silence. 'It seems that Shona's been talking—but who told you all that rubbish about my wife leaving me—who gave you the idea she'd jilted me? *That* wasn't Shona, I'll swear!'

He released one of her hands and Kelly put it to her forehead, dazed and trembling. 'No, it wasn't,' she admitted at last. 'I—I don't think anyone actually *told* me. It—it just seemed obvious. Knowing the sort of man you are and——'

'And what do you know of the sort of man I am?' he sneered. 'Why, I know more about you in two days than you could learn about me in a thousand years! For one thing, I know you've got too much imagination. You hear half a story and make up the rest—my God, Kelly, if you don't get into trouble one way you will another! Don't you realise what can happen to people who spread gossip without any idea of the real truth? I guess it's the same in your country as in mine, isn't it—the law of libel and slander?'

She gazed up at him. 'You mean, it's—it's not true?' she whispered, and he snorted his derision.

'It's about as far from the truth as we are from Trafalgar Square. And that's all I'm going to tell you—just now. Maybe when you've grown up a bit—but let's go back to your assessment of my character. It interests me—I can't wait to hear it!'

He let her go and stood back, arms folded,

watching her with a sarcastic smile on his lips. His rage seemed to have passed, but Kelly was painfully aware that it still lurked perilously near the surface. She didn't want to risk it again; but her own indignation at the way he had treated her prevented her from controlling her tongue. And after all, she might never again have such an opportunity to tell Joss Varney just what she really thought of him.

'I think you're a man who thinks only of himself,' she said slowly. 'I think you're entirely concerned with money. You're not satisfied with the wealth your companies can make for you; you want the excitement of digging it out of the ground too. I can just see you when you find gold—gloating over it like some old sourdough from the days of the gold-rush. It's like a fever—you don't do it because you *need* to. And you corrupt people like Mark with your fever, too, you feed it to them like a drug. It's—it's devil's gold, that's what it is, and I wonder just how many other lives you've wrecked with it!'

She paused, almost afraid to say more, but Joss's expression was unreadable as he nodded curtly to her to go on.

'And you think women are just toys,' she went on more boldly. 'Just there for your pleasure. All right, I don't know what really happened between you and your wife—but I'm willing to bet it was more than half your fault. And since then, you've gone around taking what you wanted and never giving anything back.' She took a deep breath. 'If you ever knew anything at all about love, you've forgotten it now. You've proved that by the way you've behaved with me.'

She stopped and watched him, her heart drumming with fear. *Could* one say such things to this arrogant, powerful man and hope to get away with them? Especially here in his own house, halfway down a Pacific cliff, with no chance of escape? Cautiously she rubbed her wrist, knowing that there would be a bracelet of bruises to show from this morning's encounter. And maybe there was worse to come. . . .

But Joss Varney made no move towards her. He stood quite still, watching her with that unfathomable expression, reminding her—as he had on her first sight of him—of a tiger, power wound up in him like a coiled spring, waiting only for release.

'And you really believe all that?' he asked softly. 'Is that why you respond the way you do when I kiss you? Because you hate me? My God, Cat's Eyes if that's the way it is, how are you going to behave when you *like* a guy? And that's the other reason I'm keeping you here—so you can learn lesson number two. I told you, you're a danger to yourself. Go around looking the way you do, dressing the way you do, and you're going to land in a whole packet of trouble—trouble you obviously can't handle.' He came closer to her and Kelly shrank away. 'You don't even know yourself, you innocent little fool. You don't even realise that under that unspotted, angelic exterior you're just about as sensual as a woman can be. You're dynamite—and it'd be a sin to let you loose on the world before you know how to cope with yourself!'

'Well, that's an excuse I never heard before!' Kelly backed away from him nervously. 'You think you're going to seduce me, don't you! Now I'm not engaged to Mark, you think I'm fair game—well, I'm not! I can fight back, you know—I haven't just got eyes like a cat, I've got the claws to go with them. And if you dare come near me again, I'll use them too—and everyone will know just what you've been doing!'

His dark eyes bored into hers and she saw the flash of his teeth as he bared them in a wolfish smile. Almost lazily, he reached out for her, and she raised her hands threateningly, determined that this time he'd be disappointed—this time she *wouldn't* respond.

And just at that moment they heard the ringing of a bell from somewhere inside the house. Joss let his hands drop to his side and Kelly, with an odd sensation in the pit of her stomach, turned her head towards the sound.

'Saved by the bell,' he said with a wry smile. 'Shona's sense of timing sure is impeccable. Lunch must be on the table.' He raised his arm and crooked it mockingly. 'Shall we go in? And we'll continue this discussion afterwards, if you still want to. But I warn you now—I'll win. I always do.'

And he was probably right, Kelly thought as she refused his arm with a toss of her head and followed him into the house. She felt exhausted; exhausted and defeated. She doubted whether she even had the energy to argue any more; and once again she wondered at Joss Varney's real reasons for keeping her here.

CHAPTER SIX

THE streets of Carmel were bathed in spring sunshine as Kelly strolled through them a few days later. It was becoming part of her routine, driving into the little town every morning. For one thing, there was the post to collect—Carmel had no delivery service and it seemed to be a local custom to call in at the post office around eleven every morning, and there was no knowing who you might see there—a lot of famous film stars and pop singers had their homes in or near the town. Kelly lived in hopes of seeing Paul Anka or Frank Sinatra queueing up for his mail. Though surely anyone like that would have sackfuls of mail to collect, and not just the few letters that came for Pacific Glade.

But then Joss would have more mail too if people knew he was here, she reflected, turning into the Plaza for a cup of coffee. He was supposed to be at the river, dredging; and in a way, she supposed, it was her fault that he wasn't.

Carmel Plaza was a small, elegant shopping complex, built in a hollow so that when you entered it from the street you were on the middle floor. On each level a covered walkway ran round the open square, with a variety of small shops selling clothes, books, sculpture, jewellery, pictures and much more—there was even a shop selling shells of all kinds, and another devoted entirely to Christmas decorations of the more expensive kind and apparently doing a roaring trade whatever the time of year.

The whole thing was open to the sky, and on the lowest level you could sit and enjoy your coffee or lunch outside, watching fountains play and admiring the flowering tubs that splashed brilliant colour everywhere.

'Hi!'

Startled, Kelly turned and saw a tall, fair-haired man hurrying towards her, coming with long strides down the steps. She smiled and waited; it was almost becoming a regular date, this, she thought with amusement—and why not? Stuart was pleasant and fun to be with. He'd been friendly from the first moment they'd met, the sort of person with whom she could feel completely at ease. And apart from Shona and her taciturn husband Andra, there was nobody else for Kelly to talk to in Carmel.

'Hi,' she said, smiling at him as he came up to her. 'I was just going to have coffee.'

'So was I. What a coincidence!' They both laughed. 'You know,' he went on, steering her to a vacant table just beyond reach of the fountain, 'I'm finding myself looking forward to eleven a.m. more and more each day. And as it gets nearer I get this awful feeling that you might not be here again—you might have gone, like a dream.'

'And would that be so terrible?' she asked

lightly, and he made a little grimace.

'Well, it could be. I mean, it's always a tragedy when a pretty girl goes out of your life—but when the pretty girl's just come from England and seems to be unattached—well!'

Kelly chuckled, but refused to be drawn. She had no intention of telling Stuart her life story. He was fun to meet and drink coffee with, but not much more. And she was still in a state of confusion over Joss and why she was still here at Pacific Glade, when she had vowed so firmly to leave at the earliest opportunity.

As Stuart went to order coffee, she gazed thoughtfully at the fountain and let her mind drift back. Back to that first day, when she and Joss had quarrelled and he had told her that she was too innocent and dangerous to let loose on the unsuspecting American public. She hadn't really understood what he meant—it seemed like an excuse for seduction to her—but later that day, after Shona's lunch and a lazy afternoon by the swimming-pool, when for some reason the need to get away didn't seem quite so urgent after all, he had come back to the subject again, and this time he had put it differently.

They were walking on the sands at the foot of the cliffs when he began to speak. The cliffs towered above them, raw rock at the bottom, craggy and chewed by the fierce waves; brilliant with flowers further up where the carpet of ice-plants, so typical of this coastline, draped like a brilliant carpet over the contours. Beyond that again lay the gardens of Pacific Glade, and the house, so open yet secluded. Kelly had never seen or imagined a more beautiful spot. If I lived here, she thought, I'd never want to leave it.

'I have to go away tomorrow,' Joss said then, abruptly breaking the silence, and Kelly was surprised to find that she didn't feel relieved, as she ought to be doing. But instead of analysing her feelings, she said quickly, 'Oh, you can drop me off somewhere, then,' and felt an odd pang at having to leave this idyllic spot, which was strange, considering she had been intending to do just that.

Joss stopped and stared out over the sea. The sun was just going down, an apricot glow beginning to spread across the sky and colour the blue waters.

'No, I don't want to do that,' she heard him saying, but there was no arrogance in his tone now. He spoke slowly, thoughtfully, almost as if he was talking to himself, and when she turned to him in amazement, he took her by the shoulders and said, 'Kelly, we seem to keep on getting across each other, and I don't want that. There are things I have to say to you—things we have to get sorted out—and we can only do that when we're both a bit calmer and seeing things more clearly. I'm going back to the river for a few days—my cousin's arriving in San Francisco tomorrow and I have to collect him and get things sorted out at the camp. And maybe Mark'll be coming out of hospital, he'll need transport too.'

'I don't understand,' said Kelly, feeling her body quiver under his touch. 'What things? What do you have to say to me? You've done quite enough already—' and he could take *that* any way he liked! '—there's nothing else you need do for me. In fact, if you're going to San Francisco you could give me a lift there. I was thinking of hiring a car and going touring for a couple of weeks.'

He gave her shoulders a gentle shake. 'There'll be time for that later. Believe me, Kelly, when I say there are things we have to talk about.' His eyes were intent on hers. 'Things you maybe don't know about. All I'm asking you to do is stay on here while I'm away—keep Shona company, if you like to look on it that way. You'll be free to go where you like—there's a small car in the garage you can use—and it'll be as good a part of your holiday as any. You could spend time in worse places, you know!'

Kelly had already realised that. But she looked doubtfully at him, uncertain of what to make of his offer; was it just another attempt at seduction? Because she was sure that every time she looked at Joss Varney, every time he touched her, he was well aware of the effect he was having. Well aware of the trembling of her limbs, the fluttering in her stomach. And what man would pass up such an obvious opportunity? What man of Joss Varney's type anyway, she thought ruefully.

'Look, I shan't even be here,' he insisted. 'And when I come back, we'll have our talk and if you want to go then—why, nobody'll stop you. Now what's wrong with that?'

'Nothing,' she was forced to admit. 'It—it's very kind of you.'

'So you'll stay?'

'Well—all right.' Her eyes were huge as she looked up at him, huge and green, reflecting the colour of the sea. For a long, timeless moment, their glances held; then he leaned forward and brushed her lips with his. The now-familiar surge of feeling swept her body, so that she longed suddenly for him to take her in his arms and press her fiercely against him. She felt a gnawing ache deep inside her. She wanted him to lay her down on the soft sands, cover her body with his, kiss her eager flesh and take possession of her, of every secret, intimate part of her. She yearned for him to take what he had called her 'proud virginity' and give her womanhood in return. She wanted to be his; utterly and completely his.

Her body trembled with the desire she was at last admitting to herself. Bewildered, she stared into the dark eyes that held hers with such magnetism. How could she possibly feel like this about a man she hated?

And then she knew the truth. And she turned away, knowing that there was no escape from it.

Oh *no*, she thought as she stood helpless under his gaze. No, no, *no*! I've fallen in love with him. . . .

She thought of this now, sitting at the little table in the sunshine in Carmel Plaza and waiting for Stuart to bring the coffee. The realisation had come as a complete shock to her, and even now she couldn't fully take it in. How *did* you fall in love with a man who had never been anything but brutal and overbearing? A man who was physically attractive—magnetic might be a better word—but who seemed to use that masculinity like a weapon, brandishing it in the face of her inexperience.

Kelly couldn't understand herself. She only knew that once she had acknowledged the depth of her feeling for Joss Varney, a whole lot of other things had become clear. The reason why she wasn't more upset about Mark, for instance; and the reason why she felt weak whenever she met that dark brown glance or heard the tones that could be silky or harsh. . . .

'Coffee for a lovely lady,' announced Stuart, putting two steaming pottery mugs on the table. 'And I took the liberty of ordering a piece of carrot cake, too. You were saying yesterday that you hadn't tried it yet.'

'I wonder everyone in America isn't as fat as a barrel,' Kelly declared, picking up a fork to attack the dark, fruity slab of cake, covered with cream. 'Mm—you know what it's like? Christmas pudding! Don't you have that here?'

That started them on a discussion of American and British foods which lasted through two mugs of coffee. Stuart had been to London once, but hadn't penetrated farther, and she regaled him with descriptions of Welsh cakes, Devonshire cream, Scottish oatcakes and Yorkshire pudding, until he begged her to stop.

'I shan't want to eat another thing until I've tried some of those,' he said, but Kelly shook her head vigorously.

'American food's marvellous too! It's so imaginative. Do you know, for lunch yesterday I had a three-decker sandwich filled with turkey and ham, the whole thing lightly fried and dusted with icing sugar, of all things! We'd never think of doing that at home, but it was delicious. It's the mixture of sweet and savoury that makes it so American, I think.'

'And what about today?' Stuart asked. 'What's today's lunch menu?'

'Oh, I don't know. Shona's out, so I said I'd get myself something light. Honestly, after breakfast and then coffee here I don't really need anything—but somehow I always find room, everything's so delicious.'

He leaned forward. 'So you don't really have to go back for lunch at all? Well, why not come with me? We could go down the coast and have a picnic. Get some food here, and take off—how about it?'

Kelly hesitated. The thought of Joss kept coming into her mind—but he wouldn't be home today. He hadn't said just when he'd be back, but she knew it would be several days. Meanwhile, it could be fun to go out with Stuart. She hadn't been down the coast yet, and she'd heard it was beautiful. Why not?

'Yes, I'd love to,' she said, and he smiled.

'Let's go along to the cheese shop and stock ourselves up, then. They have some really nice French bread there—you know, those long sticks? And their selection of cheeses is out of this world!'

And in that he was right, Kelly thought as she stood beside him before the array of cheeses on the counter and in tall glass-fronted cupboards behind it. Cheeses she'd never heard of, cheeses of all nationalities. The man serving them seemed to be blessed with endless patience, too; he gave them sample after sample, cutting off small pieces and putting them on crusty French bread before popping them into Kelly's mouth. Laughing, she protested at last and held up her hand.

'I shan't need any lunch at this rate! Look, I like that one, the one like a Brie. Is that all right?' she asked Stuart.

'Fine by me,' he smiled, and the man serving them nodded approvingly.

'That's an amazing cheese,' he told them. 'Only came in this morning and—why, I could eat it all day. In fact, I probably will!' He cut a generous piece and weighed it up. 'And a French stick? You've chosen your wine already, I see—couldn't be better. A meal fit for a king.'

Kelly laughed and agreed. She took the cheese and followed Stuart from the shop, and they strolled together through the Plaza and back to Stuart's Alfasud.

'Where are you parked?' he asked, and nodded

when she told him. 'It'll be all right there till we get back. Now, here's for the open road!'

Kelly sat beside him, enjoying the wind in her hair. The car Joss had lent her was a small saloon—a compact, they called them here. It was automatic, and Kelly enjoyed driving it, but she was still nervous about driving on the right and hadn't ventured farther than Carmel. Now she looked eagerly about, thrilled by the coastline with its spectacularly rugged cliffs washed by surging, foam-topped waves.

When would Joss be back? And what was going to happen when he came? Kelly shivered, excitement pulsing through her veins as she remembered that last evening. He hadn't done what she wanted down in the cove, but maybe that was just as well. Instead, after his brief kiss, he had drawn her arm through his and they had sauntered along the sands, watching the sunset and listening to the gulls screaming overhead. Then they had climbed the steps back to the garden and stood on the terrace together, looking down over the flame-coloured sea and sipping long, cool drinks before dinner. The air was shrill with crickets and a few nightbirds called. Earlier, Kelly had seen her first humming-bird here and the magic of the moment was still with her.

Joss had said very little then, or during dinner, but his silence was of a different quality from the grim taciturnity she had experienced before. She had longed to hear what he had to say, but knew it was no use asking. Already she was aware that

when Joss Varney said something, he meant it.
So just what did he mean now? What *was* he going
to say when he came back from the river?

Could it possibly be that he loved her, too?
That under the fighting his own feelings had been
growing in spite of himself? That he saw her now,
not as a foolish child, but as a woman?

He was attracted to her, she already knew that.
Nothing else could explain the passion in his
kisses, in the hard tautness of his body, in his
arms and hands when he held her. But he might
be equally attracted to any woman. He was a sensual man.

Kelly had longed for him to tell her. She had
waited for him to come to her room that night,
her heart beating fast because she knew that if he
did she wouldn't be able to refuse him, wouldn't
want to. But he hadn't come. And when she woke,
late next morning, he had gone.

So it was a good idea to come out with Stuart
today. It would pass the time, help her to get
through a few more aching hours until Joss
returned.

They ate their lunch on a tiny shelf of grass
halfway down the cliff, watching the ocean hurl
itself against the crags and reefs and islets that
showed dark and dangerous just off the shore. As
Kelly had expected, the meal was delicious. The
bread was crusty and light, the cheese soft enough
to spread over it, and the wine that washed it
down made her feel pleasantly sleepy; afterwards,
they ate sweet juicy Californian oranges. Then

they lay back and dozed peacefully, the roar of the waves below making a pleasant background music.

'How long are you staying round Carmel, honey?' Stuart asked lazily.

'I don't know. Not long.' But she hoped she would be.

'Known him long? The great tycoon?'

'No, not really.' Even if it did feel like half a lifetime. 'I don't know a lot about him at all.'

'No? Well, you would if you stayed around here long. All the high spots of Joss Varney's life seemed to happen around Carmel. Funny, when you think he originally came from Alaska and spends a lot of time in Seattle. But it's here he seems to meet his fate!'

Is it indeed? Kelly thought, and tried to quell a quickening of her heartbeat when she thought maybe *she* could be the next high spot. But instead of saying what she thought, she enquired casually: 'Do you know him well?'

'Only slightly. We meet at parties, that sort of thing. I'm not really his kind, you know!' Stuart chuckled. 'I like the good life too much! Joss is too keen on hard work for me. What I say is, if you can afford to enjoy life, why not? But I know about him, of course. I mean, it's like a village here. You can't hide much.'

Kelly badly wanted to ask Stuart more—there was so much she wanted to know about Joss—and she searched for words before finally asking: 'Did you know his wife at all?'

'Cassie? Sure, everyone knew Cassie. She was a local girl—well, lived a bit down the coast from here, but like I say it's a real sort of village. Yeah, we all knew Cassie. Better'n Joss did, most of us, I reckon.'

'How do you mean?'

Stuart shrugged. 'Well, Joss had only just started coming here a lot. Cassie'd been around all her life, we'd watched her grow up. We all knew she was still a kid, had a lot of growing up to do—she wasn't ready for marriage. But Joss saw her as a woman and he fell like a ton of bricks. Couldn't rest till he'd made sure of her, and that meant marriage. Anyone could have told him it wouldn't work out,—but Joss wouldn't have listened.'

No, he wouldn't, Kelly thought. He hadn't changed in that respect, then.

'Well, of course it was disaster. I guess they tried over and over to patch it up. Maybe they'd have succeeded too, after the baby came—but poor Cassie never saw the kid. She died the day after it was born.'

Kelly felt her body turn cold. A baby! And Cassie had *died*! She thought of the things she'd said to Joss and put cold hands to her cheeks. No wonder he had been angry! She was only surprised that he hadn't thrown her out there and then.

'The—the baby?' she asked in a faint voice. 'What happened to the baby?'

'He died too,' Stuart told her briefly.

'Premature, apparently, and pretty small. There may have been something wrong with him too, I don't know.'

The sad little story left Kelly stunned. A young marriage gone wrong—the attempt to patch it up with a baby—and the tragedy that had resulted, with both mother and baby dead. Why—why?

No wonder Joss Varney was embittered. No wonder he had been against young marriages, and tried to warn men like Mark against them. Her heart went out to him and she made a silent vow that if—*if*—he was coming back to tell her that he loved her, then she would make up for everything. Young she might be, but she was mature enough, surely, to take on this lonely, unhappy man and make him laugh again. Teach him to love life. Maybe she had begun already, she thought, remembering the quiet companionship they had shared on the terrace that last evening, the soft kiss he had given her on the beach. *That* hadn't been the Joss Varney of the mountains, forcing her to lie close to him in the tent, his hands hard and brutal. And she felt her cheeks grow warm at the memory of that night.

'I'm going to have to take you back now, honey.' Stuart's voice broke into her thoughts. 'Even I have to do *some* work—though not more than I can help. Got a date with an architect this afternoon, over in Monterey. Mind if we go along now?'

'No, of course not.' Kelly scrambled to her feet. 'It's been lovely, Stuart. Thank you.'

'Thank *you*.' He made a mock bow. 'We'll do it again. And maybe you'd like to come out with me tomorrow evening? Party I'm going to. You'd enjoy it.'

Kelly hesitated. Joss might be home by then. 'Can I let you know?' she asked.

'Sure. I'll give you a ring. Hope you can make it—you'll meet some real nice people.'

'If they're your friends,' she said smiling at him, 'I'm sure I will.'

As she settled herself in the car, her mind went back to Joss. Both Shona and Stuart had implied that the marriage to Cassie had been some time ago. But Joss was a virile, sensual man, she knew that. Surely there had been other women?

'He's never thought of marrying again, then?' she enquired, trying to keep her voice casual, and Stuart, manoeuvring the car carefully back up the track to the road, answered absently: 'Well, I don't really know. There've been plenty of women, of course—after the first year or so. He seemed to go back into his shell for a bit, then when he came out he came with a bang. But nobody serious, that I knew of.' He paused to let a car go by before emerging into the road. 'Except for Damask, of course.'

'Damask?' Something about the name and the way Stuart spoke it seemed to strike at Kelly's heart. 'Who was Damask?'

'*Is*,' Stuart corrected her. 'Damask very much *is*. Well, she's been around for a long time now. A lot of people thought she and Joss would make a go of it—oh, it would have been about eighteen months after Cassie died. Damask was there from the beginning—she knew Cassie, knew 'em all— but after a while folks gradually realised there didn't seem to be any other woman around Joss Varney. The others kind of disappeared. And he and Damask were obviously very close.'

'Oh.' Kelly tried to imagine Damask. The name conjured up a sultry beauty, someone who would match Joss's vibrant good looks.

'She was older than Cassie, you see, nearer Joss's age. I guess he could talk to her, better than the younger ones. They spent a lot of time together. And then—well, she up and married some other guy. Shook everyone, but Joss most of all, I reckon. She went off to Florida then, but I did hear she and her husband had split up lately. Last I heard, she was on some world tour.'

Kelly didn't need to hear any more. The fact that Joss and Damask hadn't married was almost beside the point—which was that Damask was certainly the kind of woman Joss admired and got on with. A rich, smouldering enchantress, a woman who shared his world of wealth and good living. A far cry from a simple English girl, with short fair hair that never went any way but its own, who earned her living by working in a public library and who felt most at ease in sweater and skirt, or T-shirt and jeans.

She had fallen deeply in love with Joss, there was no getting away from that. But had he really fallen in love with her? *Could* that be why he wanted her to stay, why he wanted to talk to her? Or was there some other reason?

Maybe she'd been kidding herself all along, Kelly thought sadly as she got out of Stuart's car and thanked him again for the picnic.

'It's been fun,' he said, smiling at her. 'We'll do it again. And I'll give you a ring about that party, right?'

If only she could have fallen in love with Stuart, how much simpler life would be, she reflected.

Kelly drove thoughtfully back to Pacific Glade and parked the compact in the garage, beside Joss's grey Porsche. She stood outside the house for a moment, looking wistfully around her. For a few days, she had allowed herself to dream. Now, even though Damask didn't appear to be a real threat, the mention of her had opened Kelly's eyes. How *could* she have supposed that a man like Joss Varney could be attracted to her? It was just as she had originally imagined, she told herself miserably. He had been embittered by his first marriage and now he was cynical about all young marriages—and particularly about young women. He seemed to have an urge to destroy all romantic illusions, and together with his blocking off of all real emotion in himself, so that he could see women only as sex objects, that could only mean one thing.

I must get out of here, Kelly decided. Every moment I stay is a risk. Because if he does come back and tries to seduce me, I'm not going to be able to resist. And if he knows I love him, then there's no hope for me, no hope at all.

Her mind made up, she walked briskly into the house and went straight to the phone.

The house was still silent as Kelly, clad only in a silk robe and carrying a towel, wandered into the big living-room. Shona and Andra were away for the day, she knew, visiting Andra's brother in Monterey; they wouldn't be back until late. The house was empty and the only sounds were those of the sea, surging restlessly round the rocks below.

Kelly had debated going for a swim in the cove, but remembered that Joss had warned her against doing so alone; sometimes, he said, you could get a huge wave, a 'king', from even the calmest sea, and be swept far out before you knew what was happening. The swimming-pool had looked inviting too. But suddenly she knew that what she wanted most of all was a jacuzzi.

The water was warm in the blue pool by the window. Kelly slipped out of her robe and stood, naked and slender, on the edge. Normally she would have worn a bikini, but with the house empty there was no need. She slipped into the silky water and closed her eyes in bliss as the whirlpool action sent bubbles racing across her body, setting up a tingling sensation all over her. It was like bathing under a waterfall, she thought, lying back and letting herself float in the surging water. The gentle but persistent massage refreshed her, soothing away her cares and leaving her feeling relaxed and free.

She didn't know how long she'd been there when a sound jerked her eyes sharply towards the door. Her heart seemed to stop momentarily, then started up again, kicking wildly as she found herself staring at Joss Varney. He was standing by the rail that separated the jacuzzi from the rest of the room, and he was watching her, his expression completely unreadable.

'Oh! I—I didn't know you were coming back today!' Kelly sought frantically for cover, but there was none. 'Don't—don't stand there staring at me like that!'

'Why, how would you like me to stare at you?' He came round the rail and threw himself down in a lounger. 'It's not every day I come home to find a mermaid in my hot tub. Did you get washed up by the ocean . . .? No, I didn't let anyone know I was coming. It was a sudden decision.'

'Is everything all right at the camp?' she asked faintly. It was ridiculous to be talking like this when she was naked in a bath, but she had to keep things normal somehow. . . . And she noticed now that he too was wearing a robe, a white towelling one that accentuated his tan. He must have been intended to use the jacuzzi as well! She glanced around for her towel, but it was out of reach. Unless he would hand it to her—and she had a strong feeling that he wouldn't—she was stranded here.

'Things are just fine,' he said in a tone that meant they weren't. 'The river's running high—

gold rushing past every minute, straight down to the next claim. But I got my cousin installed with another guy and they're getting down to it now. It means I'm losing out, though, having to share three ways.'

'And of course, that matters terribly, doesn't it,' she said quickly. 'I mean, you can't really afford to lose that money, can you? I wonder you came back at all.'

His dark eyes were on her, raking her body which he must be able to see clearly through the translucent water. She turned sideways in an attempt to hide herself and wished desperately that she had put on a bikini after all.

'I came back because I had to see somebody,' he said slowly, and stood up. Paralysed, Kelly watched as he slipped off the robe and, all in one movement, slid into the water. She saw just enough to realise that he too was naked, then she was scrambling out over the side of the pool.

'Oh no, you don't!' A hand came out of the water and grasped her ankle, jerking her back. She fell into his arms and gasped as she felt his flesh against hers. His thighs were long and hard against her own, and his hands roamed possessively over her body. Her blood surged in time with the jacuzzi bubbles then she felt herself being twisted round in his arms so that they lay together in the gushing water. As his lips came down on hers Kelly felt her resistance melt away. Her arms stole up round his neck and she moved closer, wanting to feel every inch of his skin against hers.

He wrapped her closely to him, his fingertips exploring the curves of her body. Letting her lips go, he dived his head beneath the water to continue his exploration with his mouth while Kelly arched her body towards him invitingly, instinct taking over from inexperience, knowing by her own delight that she was pleasing him too.

'Kelly,' he muttered, surfacing again. 'My God, Kelly, did I say you were dynamite—here, let's get out!'

He lifted her from the water and placed her on the Italian tiles. Then he was out himself, carrying her over to the fur-covered sofa. Gently, as if she were made of porcelain, he laid her down and knelt beside her, running his hand silkily over her wet skin.

'Do you want to be dried first?' he muttered huskily. 'Or shall we stay wet . . . my little mermaid of the ocean. . . .'

Kelly tried to speak, but her voice had deserted her. She wanted to say that, wet or dry, she needed him. She wanted to tell him that he was right, she had never felt this way with Mark, couldn't imagine feeling it. Turning towards him, she slid one arm round his neck and let her other hand trace a path down through the wet hairs of his chest. His eyes darkened and he crushed his body against hers and lowered his mouth to her breast. His lips were like fire on her skin and a wave of desire shook her. She had just begun to make her own tentative journey of exploration when the telephone rang; and although they tried to ignore it, the insistent sound brought them both reluctantly back to reality.

'Damn!' Joss looked for the first time uncertain, glancing from her to the telephone. Then he seemed to make up his mind and gathered her close again, his lips urgent. But the telephone went on ringing, and to Kelly's dismay the magic had vanished.

'It doesn't matter,' he murmured against her throat, but she wriggled out of his arms and whispered: 'But it might—it might be important.'

He sighed and, with an air of humouring her, lifted the receiver and spoke into it.

Kelly, watching him, felt suddenly uneasy. Joss's expression had changed. He glanced at her, his eyes suddenly cold. She saw the dawning anger, the contempt, and she cringed in bewilderment against the fur. Who was it—what was making him look like that?

As soon as he put down the phone, she knew. His face thunderous, he stalked back to the jacuzzi, returning to throw her towel over her; his own was already knotted round his waist.

'Obviously it *was* important,' he said harshly. 'Your new boy-friend, Stuart—thanking you for a great day, and saying he'd pick you up at eight tomorrow for the party!'

CHAPTER SEVEN

'WELL, *you* didn't take long to get fixed up,' Joss snarled.

Kelly lay on the sofa, hardly aware of the damp fur beneath her. Her body was still warm from his embrace, still burning from the trail his lips had left over her breasts. Her blood still pulsed through her veins, her flesh was still eager to welcome him. And yet, in the few short moments he had taken to answer the phone, everything else had changed. He had discovered her friendship with Stuart and she didn't know why it should make him angry, but now that it was in the open she would do her utmost to defend herself.

'What do you mean?' she demanded hotly, pulling the towel more closely round her, her face burning as she recalled the last few minutes. 'Stuart's a friend, nothing more.'

'Stuart's the biggest Casanova in Carmel, that's all!' he threw back at her. 'A different girl every week, that's our Stuart——'

'And you don't approve?' she asked stingingly. 'I thought it was just exactly *your* philosophy. Wasn't that what you encouraged Mark to do? Isn't it what you do yourself?'

'That's got nothing to do with it!' Joss

snapped, but Kelly was ready with her own retort.

'I think it's got everything to do with it! You're nothing but a womaniser! You think they're all for you, all the girls, and you just don't like the idea that someone may have got there first.' Too late, she realised the implication he was bound to put on her words, but she couldn't draw back now.

'Like I said, then,' he said, his voice silky and dangerous, 'it didn't take you long to get fixed up.'

'No, it didn't.' If she'd given him the wrong idea, that was just too bad. Or maybe it was all to the good after all; if he thought Stuart had pipped him to the post, he might lose interest in her, leave her alone. And she only had to get through the next two days before the hire car she had rung up for was ready. She could, in fact, have had one right away, but it would have been a large one and Kelly didn't feel able to cope with a big American car. She had agreed to wait a day or two until a compact became available.

She glanced up at Joss and was shaken by the expression in his eyes. She had seen that fury blaze there once before, when she had put her foot in it over his marriage. Oh yes, she'd been wrong sure enough to imagine that he might love her. Sex, that was all he was after; an easy roll with an inexperienced young English miss, who would go away afterwards, back to England where she couldn't be a nuisance to him.

She thought with shame of the way she had behaved, the way she had responded to his touch, and she knew she couldn't let that happen again. From now on, she must keep well out of Joss Varney's reach, or she would never be able to live with herself again.

'All right,' she said boldly, 'so I've been seeing Stuart. That's my business, isn't it? It's nothing whatever to do with you.'

'I'd have thought it was everything to do with me,' he said, his voice thick with anger. 'Or maybe now you've found out about men and women you practise with every man you meet? Maybe you're getting a taste for variety, even this early in your career——'

The crack echoed round the room as Kelly sprang to her feet and slapped his face with all the force she could muster. The towel slipped away from her body and she grabbed wildly for it, then backed away round the sofa. Joss stared at her for a moment, his face white under the blow, then reddening. Then he began to move in.

'No!' Kelly gasped, terrified, trying with one hand to retain her towel, with the other to keep the sofa between them. 'Don't—don't touch me! I won't let you—I don't want you——'

'What you want,' he gritted, 'has precious little to do with anything. I know better than you do what you want at this precise moment, Kelly Cat's Eyes—and it's *this*!'

He had her by one arm, dragging her inexorably

back towards him. Kelly twisted and squirmed in
his grasp, frantic to get away, but his fingers were
like steel round her wrist. She felt him pull her
body hard up against his, felt the dampness of his
chest through the towel she still clutched round
herself and then, as she flung back her head to
protest, felt her mouth silenced as his came down
on it, crushing all the defiance from her as his
lips bruised hers with a ruthlessness and force that
terrified her.

The kiss lasted only seconds, but it left Kelly
shaken and humiliated. The tenderness and passion that had called forth such an eager response
from her earlier had vanished. She was left with a
sensation of being battered by a sheer animal
power she could only half understand. Almost
afraid to meet his eyes, she glanced up through
quivering lashes at him. Then, almost visibly
gathering his control, Joss dropped his arms away
from her and stepped back. His eyes burned in a
livid face and he was breathing quickly, but he
clearly had himself in hand again as his glance
seared her trembling body.

With a stifled cry, Kelly turned away and flung
herself on the sofa, her bitter tears flowing on the
damp fur. For a while, she was aware of Joss still
standing there, staring down at her. But she didn't
look up; she felt that she would never be able to
face him again. And when, at last, her sobs died
and she raised her head and stared with reddened
eyes around the room, he had gone.

Slowly, Kelly got up and found her robe,

wrapping herself in it. The waters of the jacuzzi lay still and clear again, but she could scarcely bear to look at it. She left the big lounge and went up to her own room, closed the door and leaned back on it.

She knew now that she ought to have left before—the first day she was here. After all that had happened, she couldn't imagine why she had stayed. How had Joss Varney managed to persuade her that he was safe, that he wished her well? Her own first instincts had been right—she ought to have steered well clear of him from the beginning.

He'd been right too, of course. She *was* too young and innocent—at least, for a man like him. She couldn't cope with his aggressive masculinity. Totally inexperienced, she didn't have any idea how to handle the passion—the *lust*—that seemed so near the surface in him. And in herself, too, when he was around. That was the most frightening thing of all. The feeling that, even now, he would need only to touch her, to bend his lips towards hers, for her to be melting in his arms again, swept by the desire that was so alien to what she really wanted yet took her over so completely.

It mustn't happen again. There must be no possible chance of its happening again.

Kelly finished drying her still-damp body and slipped into a turquoise caftan that flowed loosely round the lines of her figure. She sat by the window, gazing out over the Pacific, watching the

sunset and thinking sadly of that other sunset that
she and Joss had watched together. Had it all been
a mistake, a romantic dream? It seemed as if it
must have been. And as the first stars began to
prick the deepening blue of the sky she felt a great
sadness overwhelm her. As if she had lost something of inestimable value; something that she
would never, ever find again.

The sky was dark and full of stars when Kelly
was at last disturbed from her thoughts by a knock
at the door.

Joss! Kelly jerked back to life like a puppet on
a string. Before she took time to think, she was at
the door, slipping the little bolt across. Then,
feeling safer, she crept back to the bed and sank
down on it, waiting breathlessly.

Joss knocked again impatiently and called her
name.

'G-go away,' Kelly answered tremulously.

'Don't be so silly,' snapped Joss, his tone exasperated. 'Look, Kelly, I've got some supper
ready. Come down and eat it.'

'I'm not hungry.'

'You will be before morning,' he retorted,
and she was reminded of the morning by the
river, when she'd knocked her bacon out of his
hand.

'I told you,' she said stubbornly, 'I'm not
hungry. I'm not coming down. Just go *away*!'

'Kelly,' he said, and his voice was grim now,
'I'm not pleading with you—I'm telling you.
Come out of there and stop behaving like a little

kid. We've got things to talk about. Now, open that door!'

Kelly said nothing. Her body began to tremble, and she wrapped her arms tightly round herself. Let him stay there all night—let him rage and storm, even plead, though she knew now he wouldn't do that. She wasn't coming out, and that was final.

'I can't think what you want to say to me that can't be said through a closed door,' she said, and her voice sounded bolder than she felt. 'You've told me enough already, I'd have thought. I'm a silly little kid anyway, so how could I possibly understand anything a big grown-up man like you might have to say?'

There was a silence then, a silence so long that Kelly began to wonder if he had gone. And then Joss said, and his voice was heavy: 'All right, Kelly, I'll leave you to it. Maybe in the morning you'll be able to see reason.' And she heard his footsteps going down the stairs.

Kelly lay down on the bed then, staring unseeingly out of the window at the darkness beyond. She'd won. She had bested Joss Varney in the battle of wits that seemed to be a permanent feature of their thorny relationship. She had defeated him.

But somehow it didn't seem a sweet victory. And she wondered unhappily just how long it was going to take her to get over her feeling for him.

The rest of her life, perhaps?

By midnight, Kelly was having to admit that once again Joss had been right—she was starving. It was a long time since her picnic with Stuart, and she had eaten nothing since then. The smell of the supper Joss had cooked had floated up the stairs, tormenting her, so that she wished heartily that she could go down and share it with him. But she had restrained herself—and that had been hours ago. The thought of holding out until morning appalled her.

Joss had gone to his room some time ago. She knew that because, owing to its position on the cliff, Pacific Glade was built on several levels. Joss's room was the highest in the house and she had heard his footsteps going up the polished stairs. They hadn't hesitated, though she had held herself rigid, expecting him to come to her door; but he hadn't, and Kelly hadn't known whether to be relieved or disappointed.

The house was silent now. Surely it would be safe to creep down to the kitchen and get herself something to eat?

Kelly opened her door quietly and, barefoot, slipped down the stairs. The kitchen door stood open and she closed it behind her before switching on the light. Then she made for the refrigerator.

It must have been a delicious supper, she noted ruefully. Pâté, a cold chicken leg and the remains of a fruit pie occupied one of the shelves, almost as if left there for her. Maybe Joss had anticipated her night raid and provided the food, intending to follow her down and catch her in the act of eating it. Well, that wouldn't work, because she was going to take it all back to her room and eat in safely! Rapidly, she filled a tray with cracker biscuits, butter, salad and the pâté and chicken. A half-empty bottle of wine caught her eye and she took that too, adding a glass and cutlery. Well, she thought, if you're going to have a midnight feast it might as well be in style!

She was just turning towards the door and glancing about to see if she had forgotten any-thing, when she saw the handle begin to turn and her heart sank.

So Joss had won again! He must have been sitting up there waiting for her to go down. And in that silent house, even the soft sound of bare feet wouldn't have escaped his sharply-listening ears.

Kelly felt like crying. She stood perfectly still, watching the door open. Oh, get on with it, she thought exasperatedly—and then relief washed over her and she began to laugh, almost hysteric-ally.

'Miss Kelly!' Shona exclaimed in shocked tones.

Kelly put the tray down on the kitchen table. It didn't matter if Joss did hear her now—he could hardly assault her under Shona's nose. 'I'm sorry, Shona,' she said weakly. 'I saw the door-handle turn and I was terrified!' And that was true enough.

'Och, I thought it was burglars!' Shona

affirmed, sinking on to a kitchen chair. 'I shouldn't have come in, I know, Andra's always telling me you should keep out of the way if anyone breaks in—but in *my kitchen*, I wasn't having that! But what are you doing, Miss Kelly? Didn't you have a meal this evening?'

Ruefully, Kelly shook her head. 'I—I wasn't hungry then.' She sat down opposite Shona and began to eat. 'But I couldn't sleep, so I thought perhaps I ought to have something. Mm—it's delicious! Did you have a nice day, Shona!'

'Aye, caught up on all the gossip. Ian's good company and it's always a pleasure to see him and Andra together.' Shona hesitated and glanced at Kelly. 'Not that all we heard was good news. I see Mr Joss is back—his truck was in the drive.'

'Yes, he came back this afternoon,' said Kelly, wondering what this had to do with gossip.

'Aye, I thought as much.' Shona sighed. 'You'd think it was once bitten, twice shy, but men are all fools, one way or another. And especially over women.' She seemed almost to have forgotten Kelly and to be talking to herself. 'Well, we'll just have to bide a while and see. Maybe it'll come to nothing.'

Kelly stared at her, her fork halfway to her mouth. 'Shona, what are you talking about?'

Shona shook her head and looked at Kelly, and Kelly was shocked to see that her eyes were bright with tears. She laid down her knife and fork and reached across to touch the old woman's hand. 'Shona, what is it?'

'Maybe I shouldn't say anything,' the house-keeper gulped. 'Andra says it's foolish to worry and there's nothing we can do anyway. Mr Joss runs his own life. But when you've seen one mistake and what it can do to a man—'

'Shona, tell me, *please!*' Kelly had made up her mind to get away from Joss. She'd told herself he could never be anything to her, that she must get far away and forget him. But she had to know what was upsetting Shona so.

'It's that other one,' Shona said at last, her mouth working as she looked at the table. 'She's come back. Been on a world tour, they said, after divorcing the man she ran away with, and now she's back, just when he was settling down, and dear knows what trouble it will cause—there's always trouble where that one's concerned.'

'You mean . . . Damask?' Kelly scarcely dared speak the name. It seemed too much of a coincidence that she should return now, just when Stuart had been speaking of her. But there was surely no one else whom Shona could mean.

The Scotswoman nodded her head bleakly. 'Aye, that's right. Damask Bentley, as she is now. She's over in Monterey this minute, staying with friends, Ian told us. But she won't be there long, not if I know anything. She'll be over here to see Mr Joss as soon as she finds he's home. *And* expecting to pick up just where she left off too, I wouldn't be surprised. As if three years' marriage

to another man, and a divorce besides, wouldn't
make a scrap of difference!'

'But surely it will,' Kelly protested. 'Surely Joss
won't—I mean, she let him down before——'

'It's to be hoped that he sees it that way,' said
Shona, her voice heavy with foreboding. 'But
who's to say? He once hinted to me that it wasn't
that way at all—that he more or less drove her
into the other man's arms. And if that's the
case . . .'

Kelly saw at once what she meant, and saw too
that it could be true. Joss, remorseful and embittered by his first marriage, might well have drawn
back from taking that final step with another
woman; might well have encouraged her to accept
another man's proposal. And now that her marriage had failed, now that she was back—well, it
was easy to see that this time he might accept her
love without reservation. Clearly, that was the
way Shona saw it, anyway.

Well, Kelly thought, taking her dishes to the
sink, at least that ought to take some of the pres-
sure off *her*. But the thought didn't come as any
relief. And she felt oddly depressed as she turned
back to Shona, still sitting at the table, and laid
her arm across the old woman's shoulders.

'Don't worry about it, Shona,' she said gently.
'I'm sure it will all turn out for the best. And, as
you say, he runs his own life now. He must know
what's best for him.' And that was something she
didn't believe. Joss Varney, Kelly was beginning
to think, saw life through very oddly-coloured

spectacles indeed. And Shona had every right to fear this new development.

As she went back to her room a few minutes later, Kelly noticed that the moon was up and shining across the top of the stairs. Just beyond its light, in the deep shadow, a figure stood watching her. But although she hesitated at her door, wondering what to do and trying to quieten the sudden fluttering of her heart, he made no sign. And after a moment she slipped into her room, not knowing why he was there nor what dreams had haunted his sleep.

Damask arrived next morning. Kelly, who slept late, woke to hear the clear, feminine voice floating up from the terrace and knew at once who it must be.

She lay back in bed, her arms thrown across her face as if to keep out the day. Of course, she ought to have known Joss didn't mean *her* when he said he'd come back because there was someone he must see. He probably hadn't even expected to find her still in residence—had most likely thought she would leave as soon as his back was turned. And, there was no doubt about it, that was what she ought to have done. Her presence now could only be an embarrassment to everybody.

Nevertheless, she would have to go down. There was no choice but to brave it out. Joss would probably be angry, Damask surprised, but there was no help for it—Kelly *had* to eat. And as she showered and dressed, she reflected bitterly on the design of the human body that made such functions so necessary. It would be very much easier to cope if food could be dispensed with!

Well, if she was going to brave it out, she'd do the job properly. Going to her wardrobe, she selected a pair of white trousers and a blue lawn shirt that made her hair look even fairer than it was. Her eyes looked back at her from the mirror, matched by the green beads she looped round her neck. The soft shirt clung to her body, accentuating her slenderness, and she added a thin gold chain round her narrow waist. The general effect was unusual and striking.

Joss and Damask were lying back in loungers, sipping coffee. Breakfast was laid on the table nearby, and Kelly went to help herself.

'So you're the little English waif,' Damask drawled. 'Joss has been telling me all about you.'

'Really?' Kelly's outward composure did not betray the turmoil she was feeling within at the sight of Joss Varney with this woman from his past. She carried her plate to a chair and sat down, glancing under her lashes at Damask.

The other girl was exactly as Kelly had pictured her. Her hair was the colour of a blackbird's plumage; it fell smoothly to her shoulders, curving under like a bell. Under its heavy fringe, her eyes were dark blue, fringed with long, sooty lashes. Her teeth flashed as she smiled at Joss, and Kelly wondered dispiritedly why she'd bothered to try to compete.

'What has Joss been saying, then?' she asked, hardly aware that this was the first time she had used his first name naturally. 'I'm surprised he calls me a waif—I'd have said *captive* myself.'

She saw Damask's eyes widen at this, and couldn't repress a glance of triumph at Joss. Clearly, he hadn't mentioned the fact that he was keeping her more or less against her will! But Joss didn't look in the least disconcerted. He smiled lazily at them both and remarked: 'Kelly's a very independent young woman. Doesn't always know quite what's best for her.' And the glance he sent her was an unmistakable reminder of the punishing kiss he'd given her yesterday evening.

Kelly's face flamed. She looked quickly at Damask and saw the older girl watching her with amusement. Almost as if she knew every detail of what had happened, Kelly thought, and wondered suddenly if Joss could possibly have been so mean. ... Yes, he could. She imagined them laughing together as he told Damask all about it. . . .

'And how do you like California?' Damask asked in her soft, drawling voice. She stretched back on the lounger, the silky material of her scarlet jumpsuit falling away to reveal slim, tanned arms.

'Very much,' Kelly answered politely. 'I haven't seen much of it yet, of course. But I'm going touring in a day or two—as soon as the car hire firm can let me have a compact.'

She risked a glance at Joss and was pleased to see that this did provoke a reaction. He was sitting up, staring at her, a frown drawing his heavy brows together.

'What's that?' he said harshly. 'You've fixed to hire a car?'

'Oh yes,' she said demurely, her heart beating fast. At least he wouldn't try anything with Damask present. 'I told you I was going to, didn't I? I arranged it yesterday. They didn't have a compact then, but they'll probably be able to let me have one tomorrow. Or even today, though I have got that date tonight. So if you don't mind, I will stay on another night. But I really mustn't impose on you any longer than that.'

The stiff little speech seemed to have more effect on him than any of her furious outbursts. His face suffused with anger and, for a moment, she was afraid he would ignore Damask's presence and remonstrate with her there and then—in his own devastating way. Warily, she shifted in her chair, ready for a quick getaway.

The tension was broken by Damask herself, who laughed suddenly. A pealing laugh that held an edge of spite in it.

'My, she's so *English*!' she gurgled. 'Isn't that sweet, Joss? I don't know how you can bear to part with her!'

'Neither do I,' said Joss, with a kind of strangled growl, and Kelly bent her head to hide a sudden nervous giggle.

All at once she felt an exhilarating sense of

freedom. She hadn't quite escaped, but there was nothing to hold her here now. Damask, who surely could not look on her as competition, was nevertheless going to make sure she was out of the way. Kelly could rely on support from *that* quarter! And she strongly suspected that it was support of a kind Jess wouldn't want to gainsay. The return of Damask into his life would made the seduction of a little English girl unimportant, even undesirable.

A shaft of pain pierced Kelly's heart at the thought. If only he *could* have loved her. Because whatever had happened between them, she knew that no other man would ever have quite the effect on her that Jess Varney had had. And life seemed a long, bleak prospect when viewed without him.

When she went away from here, she would never see Joss again. She would go away knowing that, with Damask back in his life, she could never mean anything to him. He would probably forget her before she reached Carmel in her hired compact.

In that case, the sooner she went, the better. But somehow she couldn't bring herself to make the break so easily. And there *was* that date with Stuart tonight, a date she no longer felt like keeping but would, if only to show Joss that she wasn't entirely dependent on him.

She would have this one last day. A day that she knew already would be compounded as much of pain as of sweetness; but a day she could not bear to give up.

Damask had begun to talk about her world tour, describing some of the places she had visited, and Kelly listened absently. Joss asked questions, intelligent questions that she would never have thought of herself. She could only think how she would have loved such a tour. Travel had always been Kelly's dream.

She stared out over the Pacific, trying to decide on her own tour of California, but she could think only of Joss, immaculate this morning in beige slacks and shirt that closely fitted his strong, athletic body. After his startled reaction to her announcement about the car, he had scarcely thrown her a glance—piqued, she thought, because she had made her own decision and acted on it. But no more than that; not now that Damask had arrived. Kelly was no more than a passing amusement, and if she hadn't been aware of it before, she certainly was now.

Why, oh, why, she thought miserably, did I have to fall in love with him?

It wasn't long after Shona had cleared away the breakfast things that she came out again to say that Joss was wanted on the telephone. He got up and went indoors, leaving Kelly alone with Damask.

Kelly sat quite still, looking out over the ocean. She wished she had gone indoors earlier, but it was too late now. It would be rude to get up and leave Damask at this point. She determined that as soon as Joss came back she would make her escape.

Damask, however, had no inhibitions. She began to ask Kelly questions about herself; why she had come to California, why she was now at Carmel. Kelly, increasingly embarrassed, had no choice but to answer, and soon Damask had the whole story of Mark's defection out of her.

'Say, that's bad luck,' she remarked sympathetically. 'But I don't really see why Joss brought you *here*. I mean, why not drop you off in San Francisco, you could have hired your car there and been quite free.'

'Well, that's what I wanted him to do,' Kelly said awkwardly. 'But he insisted on bringing me here. He said I—I needed a rest and he didn't like to let me go off on my own until I'd got over the flight and got used to America.' Basically true enough, she thought—at least those were the reasons Joss himself had given her. But she was well aware that he had other reasons than those. And Damask was no fool, and moreover knew Joss of old—had almost certainly been his mistress and probably would be again. She would know why Joss had really brought Kelly to Pacific Glade.

Kelly felt her face flame under the older girl's gaze. She wished Joss would come back, so that she could escape. But his call seemed to be taking a long time.

'So you don't know a lot about Joss, then?' Damask probed. 'You don't know, for instance, that he was married once?'

'Oh, yes,' Kelly said, too quickly, 'I know about

Cassie.' Well, if Damask was going to suspect *her* of becoming his mistress in the short time they'd known each other, she might as well have some grounds for her suspicion! A small imp seemed to enter Kelly. Let Damask think what she liked! Kelly herself would be away from here in a day or so. She would never see them again—how could it matter what they thought?

Damask's beautiful eyes widened. 'Oh, you do? I'm rather surprised at that. Joss doesn't usually talk freely about himself—not to strangers, anyway.' Her tone put Kelly positively in her place. 'And did he tell you about Robert, too?'

'Robert?' For a moment, Kelly was at a loss. Then she said cautiously: 'The baby, you mean?'

Damask looked put out and Kelly congratulated herself on a lucky guess. 'Yeah, that's who I mean,' the American girl said shortly. 'The little boy—the idiot child.'

Kelly stared at her. '*Idiot* child? But that—that's a dreadful thing to say!'

'It's the correct term for him.' Damask's voice was cold, indifferent. 'Joss knows it as well as anyone else. Why else do you think he would have put the brat in a home and never seen him again? Why else would he pretend the kid never existed?

'Did he—do that?' Kelly asked faintly.

'Sure he did. The kid died a few weeks later, and his father had never been near him.'

Damask's words had shed a new light on Joss's character. No doubt they'd been intended to, Kelly thought. Damask had clearly summed her up very accurately and known just what would upset her. As a warning-off, it was very effective indeed.

Politeness was the last thing in Kelly's mind as she stood up and said abruptly: 'Excuse me. I promised to help Shona this morning,' and, trembling, left Damask alone on the terrace.

Not that Damask seemed to mind. When Kelly left the terrace, she was smiling to herself; triumphantly.

CHAPTER EIGHT

BACK in her room, Kelly began to pack her clothes. It was early to be doing that, she knew, when she wasn't leaving until next day, but somehow it gave her some comfort. By this time tomorrow, perhaps, she would be away from here. Away from Damask, with her possessive attitude, away from Joss who seemed more than content to be possessed. Away from that disturbing influence that was causing Kelly more pain than joy, and confusing her senses.

How could she have fallen in love with such a man? A man bitter and cynical in his dealings with women and clearly as callous about his own child. There could be no happiness for her with such a man. So why had he got under her skin, into her blood, filling her thoughts and dreams in a way that Mark never had?

Glancing out of the window, Kelly saw that Joss had come out on to the terrace again. He was carrying bathing things and was bending over Damask, who laughed up at him from her lounger. Then, as Kelly watched, Damask's arms slid up round his neck, drawing him down to her, and the low gurgle of her laugh floated up through the clear air.

Kelly turned back into the room. She could

hear their voices, more faintly now; perhaps they were going down to the beach. Suddenly compelled, she ran back to the window and saw them disappearing down the steps. So the way was clear. And she knew then that this was her chance. She *had* to get away at once. No longer could she stay and watch Damask tighten her hold on the man she loved. She had promised herself this one last day, knowing it would be painful, but the pain was proving more than she could bear.

This might be her only opportunity. Glancing quickly out of the window again, she hurried down the polished stairs and into Joss's study. The telephone stood on his desk and she grabbed it and dialled the number of the car hire firm.

If only they had a car ready today, she prayed as she waited for the answer. If only she could get away at once, while Joss was on the beach—get right away from here, up into the sierras where he would never find her. She remembered the brochure she had brought from Mawani—the pictures of King's Canyon Park, the serenity of the giant sequoia glades. Perhaps there she could find peace and forget Joss Varney and the tumult he had caused her emotions. . . .

But there was no compact available today, a regretful voice informed her. Tomorrow, yes, she could have one first thing. It would be delivered before she was out of bed, probably. No apologies needed for her impatience. She was welcome. And the voice, cheerful and uncomplicated, rang off with an injunction to have a nice day.

'Thank you,' Kelly said mechanically, and put down the phone. She stood for a moment staring blindly at the maps on the wall, then turned dejectedly towards the door. So she was doomed after all—doomed to spend this last day in the company of Joss and Damask. . . .

'Still trying to run out on us, huh?' said Joss, from the doorway.

Kelly gasped and leaped back as if she'd been stung. 'How long have you been there?'

'Guilty conscience?' Smiling cruelly, he moved in towards her, blocking her escape. 'I guess you must want to get away from here pretty badly.'

'Yes, I do! I want to get away from you—from everything. I can't *wait* to get away, and you've no right to keep me here.' She lifted her chin defiantly and looked him in the eye. 'It's getting pretty near to kidnapping; had you realised that? You brought me here against my will in the first place, and now you won't let me go. I think the police might be interested to hear about what you've been doing, Mr Varney!'

To her intense annoyance, he threw back his head and laughed at that. She watched impotently until he controlled his mirth; then he said, amusement still colouring his tone:

'You really think so? When you've been wandering around Carmel for the last three mornings? Did you give any hint of this *captivity* to young Stuart when he took you picnicking yesterday? Or when he made a date with you to go to a party tonight?'

Kelly bit her lip. As usual, he was right. Not that she'd have contacted the police anyway—but it didn't help her morale to realise she was making a fool of herself.

'Look, I'm not keeping you here if you really want to go,' Joss said quietly. 'You can go any time you want—but I'm not helping you, either. Now, you know what a climb it is to the top of the cliff and the main road. You know just how far it is to walk into Carmel. If you want to go, and take all your luggage with you, you can go right now, okay? I shan't lift a finger to stop you.'

'You know I can't do that!' she flared. 'Oh, why are you making me stay here? Why? You've got *her* now—what can you want with me, now she's come back?'

'Oh, so you know all about her too,' he commented. 'Well, we have been the busy little bee, haven't we? And I suppose you think she's come back to claim her old lover—maybe to marry him this time, huh? *Is that what you think?*'

He shot out the last sentence, at the same time grasping Kelly's arms and shaking her ruthlessly. She cried out, and kicked furiously at his shins, but he held her away from him and when she looked into his face she saw rage there.

'Oh, please let me go!' she begged. 'Please! What does it matter what I think! What am I to you? I'm nothing—nothing. You didn't even know me a week ago—what do you want with me now? Please—*please*—let me go. . . .'

He held her against him and she saw his eyes

darken until they looked almost black. His face was perfectly still except for a tiny, twitching muscle just in front of his ear. Through her thin shirt, she could feel the steady beat of his heart; her own pulses raced under his fingers.

'You really mean that?' he murmured close to her ear. 'You really want me to let you go?'

Kelly closed her eyes. Another moment and she'd be beyond resistance. And every time that happened, she found herself more deeply involved, and more thoroughly confused. She couldn't afford to let it happen again—she *couldn't*!

'Yes,' she whispered, her voice a mere thread. 'Yes, I do. Please let me go.'

His fingers loosed so abruptly then that she staggered and almost fell against the desk. Clinging to it, she looked up in mute appeal at Joss. But there was no answering sympathy, no warmth in his expression. His face was shuttered, cold, indifferent. And she should have been glad—but instead she felt like crying.

'I'm sorry,' he said bleakly. 'I thought we had some unfinished business to settle. I was wrong.' He turned away from her and stared up at one of the maps, tracing the line of a river with his forefinger. 'Did you manage to fix a car?' he asked, almost absently.

'Yes, for tomorrow.' Her voice was subdued.

'I see. Well, that's fine. And we'd better make the most of your company today, hadn't we?' He turned back towards her and his eyes were like stones. 'You'll be coming down the beach with us, then. I came back to fix a picnic lunch, it's so warm and pleasant down there. Shona will probably have it ready by now and I expect she'll have put in plenty for three.'

'Oh, I don't think——' Kelly began, but he silenced her.

'No question of it, Cat's Eyes. You've nothing else to do. Not until—eight, is it, when your escort arrives? You mustn't miss the party, you know. Parties in Carmel are something different.'

Kelly subsided. This new, cold Joss was even more frightening than Joss in a fury. Submissively, she followed him out of the study and into the kitchen, where Shona handed them a picnic basket. Then they left the house and went down the cliff steps to the beach.

One more day. It wasn't so long . . . was it?

Down on the beach, they found Damask clad now in a brief bikini as scarlet as her jumpsuit. Evidently her favourite colour, Kelly thought, and it certainly suited her wild, dark beauty. Her long limbs and slim yet voluptuous body were already deeply tanned from the world cruise, and once again Kelly's heart sank. How could anyone compete with this?

Not that she wanted to any more, she reminded herself, slipping out of her shirt and trousers to sunbathe in the orange flowered bikini she had put on before coming out. The colour looked crude and obvious beside Damask's flaming scarlet, but there was nothing to be done about it.

She sat down on one of the rugs Joss had brought, and gazed soulfully out to sea.

Maybe it was just as well Damask had come. She could now see Joss for what he was. She had already known he was brutal from his treatment of herself. Now she knew that his harshness extended even towards his own child. She would be well out of it when she left tomorrow.

'Well, how about a swim before lunch?' said Joss, breaking into her thoughts. He was sitting on the other side of Damask—nearer than he need, Kelly considered—and he too was in bathing things, in his case a pair of brief blue trunks. With an easy movement, he rose to his feet and stood looking down at them.

It was impossible not to notice the strength and power of his calves and thighs. The hairs on his chest glinted brown and gold in the sunlight; muscles rippled under the skin of his back and shoulders. Kelly felt the old weakness at the pit of her stomach, and closed her eyes. She was just going to have to fight it! Not only today, when he was here with her, but tomorrow and all the following days, when she was missing him, aching for him. . . . Surely she would get over it eventually? Could anyone live their whole life with that dreadful, gnawing ache tearing at them? Could *she*?

'A swim!' Damask exclaimed. 'Do you know, I've dreamed about swimming from this beach at nearly every spot in the world! Sydney—Hong Kong—Paris—London—it was this place I thought of when I thought of home.' She sprang up and laid her hand caressingly on Joss's arm. 'And not just the place, either,' she added softly. 'It isn't just a place that makes home is it? It's the people who live there. . . .'

They turned together and sauntered down to the sea hand in hand. Kelly watched, the pain growing in her heart. Yet it was by her own choice. She was certain now that Joss would have taken her at any time, had she offered. *She* could have been his mistress—and then, maybe, when Damask came back he wouldn't have wanted her any more.

But in the next second she knew it was a pipe-dream. She would never have become his mistress—it wasn't her style. At least—and she recalled the sensations that had flooded her when his lips touched hers, when his hands held her body and moved so possessively on her. Yesterday, by the jacuzzi—could she honestly say she would have stopped him?

She felt again the caress of his hands, the intimacy of his touch, and shivered. They had been very close when that telephone had shrilled and changed everything. And even afterwards—she had still wanted him, and wanted him badly.

'Kelly! Come on in!'

If she did nothing else, she could act normally today. Pretend none of it mattered. Neither Joss nor Damask must ever know the way she was feeling. She'd been humiliated enough.

She got up and ran down to the sea, simulating

the carelessness she was far from feeling. The
water was cold and came as a shock, but she
couldn't stop now; she ran on in and gasped as
she fell forward and began swimming through the
white foam.

Damask and Joss were laughing at her when
she surfaced and she faced them indignantly. 'It's
freezing!'

'Well, it's still spring,' Joss reminded her. 'But
it's refreshing, isn't it? More so than a jacuzzi
bath, perhaps?' And his eyes glinted wickedly as
she tossed her head and swam away.

Now that she was over the first shock, she had
to admit the water was delicious. She had always
enjoyed swimming, and never more so than in the
sea, and for a while her cares were forgotten as
she swam and dived, revelling in the feeling of
the sun on her wet back, feasting her eyes on the
beauty of the cliffs seen from here, a riot of colour
from the ice-plants that smothered them. There
were patches of dazzling shocking-pink, cream
and yellow. In between were the more varied cul-
tivated gardens that belonged to the houses that,
like Pacific Glade, had been built about halfway
down the cliffs. Houses that looked luxurious
enough to be owned by film stars, and probably
were. It was the playground of the rich from here
all the way down to Los Angeles.

'That's enough now.' Joss's hand was on her
shoulder, and she turned quickly. The water
glinted on his brown skin as he stood waist-deep
in the water and looked at her. The magnetism

flared between them and she knew that he was equally aware of it; a gleam lit his eyes and his face changed very slightly. And then the moment was gone. He turned away, saying briefly: 'Doesn't do to stay in too long' and, keeping hold of her arm, led her firmly up the beach to where Damask was already towelling her long black hair.

Joss dried himself and pulled on a thick sweater, handing a similar one to Kelly, who couldn't restrain an inward grin at the expression on Damask's face as he did so. There was little she could say, however, since she had thoughtfully brought her own cover-up—a glamorous garment of black silk with dragons pictured on it, that Kelly guessed had come from one of the Eastern countries.

However, Damask was not one to let any opportunity slip by. She watched with amusement as Kelly pulled the bulky sweater over her head, and remarked, 'How sweet—you look even more of a waif in that!' and set Kelly's nerves tingling with annoyance.

Lunch was delicious—bread and cheese, similar to the picnic she'd shared with Stuart yesterday, together with smoked salmon, thinly-sliced turkey, salad, wine and fresh peaches, followed by coffee from flasks. Afterwards, they all lay back and dozed. And it was some time later that Kelly opened her eyes and realised she was alone.

She lay for a moment looking at the sky, then became aware that as well as the soft lap of waves on the shore, she could hear voices—Damask and Joss, murmuring quietly together. Turning her head, she saw them, sitting on a rock, their heads very close together. And Damask's hand was caressing Joss's back with slow, sinuous movements as she talked.

Kelly lay there, quite still. After that first moment she didn't want to see any more. She could guess at the intimacy of their talk by the quality of their voices; she didn't need to hear the words to know the kind of things Damask was saying in that low, husky tone, or to understand that if Joss ever spoke to *her* with that caressing murmur in his voice she would go weak at the knees.

Why did I ever come to California? she wondered dully. Mark would have written to me eventually to say our engagement was off. Why couldn't I have waited? Why am I always so impatient?

The rest of the afternoon passed without incident. The three of them formed an uneasy companionship, lazing in the sun, taking another dip in the sea, eventually packing up at sunset and winding their way back up the cliff. Kelly was uncomfortably aware that Damask resented her presence. It was implicit in a hundred little barbs that the older girl delivered, each designed to show Kelly that she was too young and simple for a sophisticated man like Joss—while Damask herself, with her beauty and experience, was just right for him. As if I didn't know that already,

Kelly thought, trailing up the steps after her. Simple I may be, but I'm not an idiot!

By the time they reached the house there was barely time for Kelly to shower and change before Stuart arrived. She chose a cream caftan of fine wool, slit up the sides and loosely gathered round the waist with her gold chain-belt, and gold high-heeled sandals to go with it. Joss had said nothing more to her about her date, though she had been dreading the moment when Stuart arrived. But as it happened, neither Joss nor Damask was about when he did, and she was able to escape without further comment.

Stuart's reaction to her appearance did a good deal to restore her morale, and she found herself, rather to her surprise, actually enjoying the evening. As Joss had told her, parties in Carmel were indeed 'something different' and she had a thoroughly good time, meeting the people Stuart laconally described as 'the locals'—many of them faces and names known to Kelly through films and pop-songs. The food, too, was delicious, and when Stuart finally took her back to Pacific Glade she felt relaxed and happy—though even then she could not quite repress her thoughts, and was aware all the time of an all too clear vision of how Joss and Damask might be spending the evening.

'It's been a great evening, Kelly,' Stuart said softly as they sat in the car just above the house, looking out over the moonlit Pacific. 'You know something—you're something different yourself.' He touched her hair. 'You've got something a lot of us out here seem to have lost. A naturalness that puts ordinary glamour in the shade.'

Kelly held her breath as his fingers moved gently down her cheek. What had Joss said about this man? That he was the Casanova of Carmel? Yet she could swear he was sincere as he went on, 'There's something else I want to tell you, Kelly. I've been involved with a lot of girls, but I've never been serious about any of them—and I don't think they have been, either. But you—well, I could get real serious about you.' He bent his head and touched her lips with his own. 'How do you feel about it, Kelly? Could you . . .?'

Kelly did not move as his kiss became more demanding. Maybe this was her opportunity to find out whether any man could stir her as Joss had done? Maybe she was the kind of woman who would respond to any kiss—and if so, perhaps she could forget about Joss, knowing that after all he was nothing out of the ordinary.

But Stuart's lips, moving expertly against her own, did nothing at all. And his hands, beginning to move over her body with increasing intimacy, filled her with a sudden and astonishing repugnance.

'No!' She twisted out of his grasp, 'No, Stuart, don't. I'm sorry—it's no good.' She looked at him appealingly.

He sat perfectly still for a moment, regaining control of his breathing. He made no move to touch her again and Kelly thought of Joss, who would certainly not have retracted so quickly. But then, she admitted ruefully, she wouldn't have wanted him to. She would have been responding, meeting kiss for kiss, straining her body against his in a wild surge of desire. . . . Well, her test—if it could be called that—had certainly proved one thing. Joss *was* the only man who could light that particular fire. And she wished heartily that it were not so.

'No?' Stuart said softly, his hand still in her hair. 'You really mean that, Kelly?'

She nodded, lowering her lashes and looking unhappily at her fingers as they twisted the cream wool of her caftan. 'I'm sorry, Stuart.'

His hand tightened a little and for a moment she was afraid he was going to persist. But then he loosed his fingers from her hair and slipped them under her chin, raising it so that he could look into her eyes.

'I'm not one to force a girl,' he said gently. 'I don't usually have to. . . . And it doesn't excite me to have a fight on my hands. But you didn't really need to tell me, anyway. It didn't work for you, did it?'

'No. I'm sorry,' she said again. 'I wish—I do *like* you, Stuart.'

'Yeah, I know. We get on. I thought maybe——' He shrugged. 'Well, that's the way the cookie crumbles, I guess. But it isn't just that, is it?' His eyes were on her, shrewd and perceptive. 'There's someone else, isn't there? And it wouldn't take too many brains to figure out who.'

Kelly felt herself flush and was glad of

the darkness. She said nothing.

'It's him, isn't it?' Stuart gestured towards the house. 'Joss Varney. The man who has everything.'

'Including Damask Bentley.' The words were out before she could stop them, and she closed her eyes. News of Damask's return did not seem to have filtered through to Carmel yet, rather to her surprise. And she had had no intention of mentioning the fact.

Stuart's eyes widened. 'Damask? Is *she* back on the scene? And out to get her claws into him again, I guess!'

'He doesn't seem to want to escape,' said Kelly, remembering the scene on the beach that afternoon; the way they had glanced round and then slipped out of sight behind some rocks. The look of cat-that's-had-the-cream that had wreathed Damask's face when they finally returned. It hadn't been hard to visualise what they had been doing, and Kelly had tormented herself for the next hour in doing just that.

'You poor kid,' said Stuart in tones of deep compassion. 'Well, I guess it'll be just as well for you to get away for a bit. Didn't you say you were planning to?'

'Yes. I've hired a car—I'm hoping to leave tomorrow. I'm going to tour for a while.'

'And I was hoping to persuade you to stay on!' He gave a rueful laugh. 'Well, I know when I'm beaten. But look here, Kelly—if ever you need a pal, I'm your man. And I mean that. Like I said, you're different.' He bent his head and gave her a kiss, a kiss of affection and friendship this time that sealed their relationship. 'You go off and enjoy your tour. And make sure you come back to Carmel when it's over, won't you? I want to make sure you're all in one piece before I take you back to 'Frisco for that plane.'

'That's kind of you, Stuart,' she said gratefully. 'I'll do that. And thank you for a lovely evening.'

He got out of the car and came round to help her out, holding her close for a moment as they stood bathed in the moonlight. 'You're a great girl, Kelly. I'm glad to have known you.'

'Oh, Stuart,' she whispered, her eyes suddenly filling with tears. 'If only things could have been different!' And when his arms began to tighten round her—'No, it's no use. I'll go now.' She reached up and gave him a last kiss. 'I'll walk down the drive from here.'

At times, she thought as she made her way down to the house, a slim, pale figure in her flowing caftan, life wasn't just unfair. It was plain cruel. And it had certainly been heaving some bricks at her just lately. Maybe California, beautiful as it was, just wasn't lucky for her. Maybe it would be better if she just cut her losses and headed straight back to England. . . .

'A touching scene!'

Kelly stifled a scream and jumped back as the door opened in front of her. She knew at once who it must be and her heart, already leaping wildly from the shock, battered at her ribcage like a bird trying to get out. Desperately, she cast a glance around, but there was no other way into the house. She would have to pass Joss to get in— and Joss, bigger than ever in the moonlight, was effectively blocking the doorway.

'Very moving,' he continued mockingly. 'Was it the beginning of a beautiful friendship—or an epilogue to something else?'

'I'm afraid I don't understand,' Kelly said coldly. 'And if you wouldn't mind letting me come in——?'

'But of course.' Sweeping an exaggerated bow, he stood aside for her to pass. 'And may I say how particularly gorgeous madam is looking tonight? Or this morning, to be accurate. Like the moon goddess herself, I thought as I saw you up there with your handsome escort. Artemis, bidding sweet farewell to Orion. That was a doomed romance too, or hadn't you heard?'

'I don't know what you're raving about.' Kelly paused at the foot of the short flight of stairs leading to her room. 'You really needn't have waited up for me, you know. I'm not a little girl.'

'You can say that again,' he murmured, his eyes moving over her body as if he was undressing her, and she flushed scarlet at the implication. Joss had clearly not forgotten the sight of her, naked, in the jacuzzi, nor the feel of her, wet and slippery, in his arms afterwards. And neither had she; the memory seared her mind every time she thought of it.

'Look, I'm sorry, but I'm going to bed—I'm rather tired and——'

His hand was on her at once, the strong fingers manacling her wrist. 'I bet you're tired. Little girl, you've had a busy day. But it's not quite over—not yet. Come here and sit down. We've still that unfinished business to settle.'

Kelly twisted and jerked her arm, but his fingers only tightened so that she had to bite her lip to stop herself crying out as he led her to the fur-covered sofa where they had lain yesterday. Unfinished business—oh, *no*! And there was little likelihood, at three in the morning, of a rescuing telephone bell. This time Joss Varney was going to get his way—whether she wanted it or not.

'Please,' she began breathlessly as he dragged her down beside him. 'Please, I——'

Joss ignored her protests. His arm was round her, clamping her firmly against his side. She could feel the heat of his body through the towelling robe he wore and the fine material of her own dress. But he didn't move, didn't speak for a moment. His gaze was fixed over the ocean, a shifting blue and silver mass under the moon.

'Artemis,' he murmured dreamily. 'She was the Greek goddess of the moon, did you know that? A virginal creature, by all acounts; didn't approve of love at all. But when she met Orion, the story was different. And she might well have succumbed to him, had she not shot an arrow into him by mistake—like the Roman Diana, she was goddess of the hunt as well. Tragic, wasn't it?'

'Strikes me she was well out of it,' Kelly muttered. 'You don't happen to have a bow handy, do you?'

'And who is your Orion?' he whispered, bending his head to hers. 'The young Lothario who took you out on the town tonight—or the poor lonely sourdough waiting at home?' His lips brushed against hers in the barest whisper of a kiss and she felt her treacherous body begin to melt. She gave a soft moan and turned her head aside, the tiny gesture of rejection taking all the strength she possessed. His hand left her wrist and she felt his fingertips slide tinglingly up her inner arm, then down from her shoulder to her breast, tightening over the swell to rub gently at her tautening nipples. A breath of sound escaped her lips and his own returned from their exploration of her neck and ears to kiss her again, demandingly this time, so that her body took over from her protesting mind and arched towards him; and her hands slid up his chest, parting the robe and flattening themselves against the hairy, muscular wall under which a heart beat as strongly and fast as her own.

He was almost covering her now and his hands slipped down her body, drawing the caftan up the length of her legs so that he could reach the naked flesh beneath. Kelly felt his fingers stroking the fine, taut skin of her inner thigh, probing and exploring until she was aware of nothing but voluptuous sensation, and she twisted and writhed in his arms, inviting him with her abandoned body to go further, to complete the exquisite and almost agonising process he'd started. Her mind seemed to stand back, reason taking second place as more ancient instincts took over and her arms and legs wound themselves around him, entwining his powerful strength and clasping it firmly to her. Together, they rocked to and fro on the thick fur, and Kelly could not tell whether the roaring she heard was that of her own tumultuous blood or the ocean pounding on the rocks outside.

Slowly Joss unwound himself from her clinging arms; slowly he sat up and looked down at her, wide-eyed and breathless in the moonlight. Then he reached down and smoothed back her hair, and his fingers trembled.

'Joss?' she whispered, and turned her head to kiss the inside of his wrist.

'My God, did I say you were dynamite?' he muttered, and let his hand trail the length of her body. 'The explosive hasn't been invented that could match you, Kelly. But it's got to stop. I didn't bring you in here for that, believe it or not. I brought you here to tell you something—just in case you go diving off in the morning before anyone can stop you.' He paused and it seemed to Kelly that his face changed, sobered. 'I've been thinking things over a lot in the past few days, Kelly. I've come to certain conclusions. And you've got to know.'

'Yes?' The room was very still as she lay there, gazing up at him. He seemed almost at a loss, ill at ease. As if what he had to say was difficult in some way—as if he thought it might change everything. At last he spoke, slowly, the words almost forcing themselves past his lips.

'I'm thinking of getting married, Kelly.'

CHAPTER NINE

'*MARRIED*!'

Kelly jerked herself upright, her eyes riveted on his face as, with hasty fingers, she dragged her caftan down round her legs. Married! It could only be to Damask—and yet he still tried to seduce her at the first opportunity.

'Look, I know it's all a bit sudden,' he went on, apparently oblivious of her reaction. 'But I wanted you to know——'

'Oh, you did?' she interrupted. 'That's mighty kind of you, Mr Varney. And so considerate, too, to tell me just *before* you actually rape me——'

'Rape?' His eyes were on her now, dark and mocking. 'I didn't notice you struggling much. In fact, if anything I'd have said you were ahead of me, little Cat's Eyes——'

'And don't call me that!' she raged. 'What sort of a man are you, Joss Varney? Some kind of wild animal? Some kind of sex maniac? Don't you have any decent feelings, any at all? Ever since I met you, you've been doing your darnedest to get me into your—your bed—and even now, when you're just about to get married, you won't give up. Don't you realise——'

'Bed? My bed?' he grated, and as he reached for her again she twisted away from him, escaping this time and placing herself securely behind the sofa. 'I was under the distinct impression you *had* been in my bed. Isn't that so? And did I take advantage of you there?'

'N-no,' she admitted, thinking of the way he had held her when they woke that first morning, in the tent. 'But ever since then——'

'Sweet Kelly,' he said, advancing towards her. 'Sweet, innocent Kelly—do you really think I couldn't have *had my way with you*, as they put it in the Victorian novels, any time I wanted? O.K., there've been a few near misses—but don't tell me you didn't enjoy them as much as I did.' His eyes slid down over her body and she knew that the caftan afforded her no protection from his memory. 'Tell me there's nothing between us,' he commanded, and his voice was low and silky. 'Tell me you're as cold as ice when I touch you—tell me my kisses don't set you alight—tell me we couldn't make a marriage like the world's never seen before, something to rival Antony and Cleopatra, something to make Romeo and Juliet look like a kids' story, something to make Paris wonder why he ever bothered with Helen of Troy. . . .'

Kelly froze where she stood, her eyes goggling as she took in his words. Marriage—to *her*? Could she possibly be hearing right? Slowly, she shook her head as if to clear it, then she heard his voice again.

'How about it, Kelly? You know we'd get along. And it would save me from the clutches of the lovely Damask.'

Kelly's head snapped up. So *that* was it? Damask, for some reason, presented a threat. And Kelly was to be the answer to that threat—a sacrifice to his arrogant desires.

'Just what is this all about?' she demanded, amazed to hear her voice apparently calm and level. 'You're not actually proposing marriage to *me*?'

'But of course. Didn't you realise?' His tones were smooth and innocent, and Kelly watched suspiciously as he moved towards the sofa. She was *not* going to let him touch her again! 'You surely didn't think——?' He paused suggestively.

'Of course I damn well thought!' she snapped. 'Damask was your mistress after Cassie died— before, for all I know—and she obviously came here meaning to be your mistress again, or maybe even your wife. What else do you expect me to think?'

'Maybe I shouldn't expect you to think at all,' he said slowly. 'Your body is so much more efficient at summing up the situation than your mind.'

Kelly caught her breath. 'That's a foul thing to say!'

'Not at all. It's quite true. Look at the way you respond to me when I make love to you. Yet as soon as your mind takes over, back comes the spitting little wildcat.' He moved nearer. 'Why not listen to the body, Kelly? It's so much wiser.'

'Don't come near me!' She backed away, edging

for the door. 'I just don't understand. Why *me*? Why have you suggested this?'

Just say you love me, she thought hungrily. Say you love me as I love you—and maybe everything will be all right. . . .

But he merely shrugged and said: 'I'd have thought it was obvious. We get along.'

'We don't!'

'Sexually, we *do*,' he insisted. 'And once we got that organised, I reckon we could have a pretty good life. Look, I'm tired of the glamour bit—the parties, the social whirl. I get that all the time up in Seattle, where I spend most of my life. It's not so bad in Alaska, but I don't get so much time there. If I married Damask, what do you think my life would be? More and more of the same. I don't want it. I come to California for a bit of quiet, some real life in the mountains, and now I'm not getting that either.' He moved closer again. 'I'm all man, Kelly. I need a woman—a woman who can satisfy me and be there whenever I need her. Damask demands too much from a guy, things I can give her but I don't get any pleasure from. You—you're different. We match.' He was in front of her now, his hands sliding sensuously up and down her sides, gradually drawing up the soft material so that he could touch her skin. 'We could have a good marriage, Kelly.'

Kelly closed her eyes. Her body was screaming at her to respond to him, to wrap him in her arms, let him carry her over to the sofa and finish what he'd started so passionately only a short time before. But this time, her mind won the battle. She drew herself away from him and now he made no effort to detain her. In his eyes she saw triumph, and she hated him for it.

'Leave me alone, Mr Varney,' she said coldly. 'I'm afraid you've made a big mistake about me. I'm not marrying you. I wouldn't marry anyone for the reasons you seem to find so convincing. Sex—lust—a woman to be there whenever you need her. What about *her* needs? This unfortunate woman you marry—doesn't what *she* wants ever come into it? You don't want a wife, Mr Varney, you want a concubine. And it's not going to be me!'

With a lithe movement she twirled away from him and was through the door and halfway up the stairs before he could move. She caught a quick glimpse of him, staring up at her, as she reached her room; then she was inside, slamming and locking the door behind her. Safe at last, she leaned against it, head drooping with a sudden exhaustion. Then, utterly weary, she made her way over to her bed and fell across it.

There was little left of the night, but Kelly was aware of every moment, and it seemed to go on for ever. By the time the sky began to pale with dawn, she had been over the scene with Joss time and time again, and she was still as baffled as ever.

Why should he suddenly decide to marry her? (As if she had no say in the matter!) Was he afraid to remain single any longer, now that Damask was back? Evidently he was no longer enamoured of his former mistress—but her undoubted sensuality, coupled with his, spelt danger. Marriage to someone else, presumably, would remove that danger.

And Kelly had been the nearest available candidate. He already knew, all too well, that she was unattached—she still hadn't forgiven him his part in that, she reminded herself—and that she was responsive to him physically. But that was all, surely? There was nothing more between them, nothing that could ensure happiness beyond the bed.

Marriage with Joss could, given the right circumstances, be paradise. But marriage in these circumstances—it would be hell. And she rolled over on the bed and groaned into her pillow as the first thin spears of dawn crept through the window and touched her with their grey light.

She must have fallen asleep soon after dawn, nevertheless, but it was still early when she woke, heavy-eyed and with a thumping head. Wearily she got off the bed and realised that she hadn't even undressed. She slipped off the caftan and went into her bathroom, wondering if there was any aspirin there.

The bathroom window overlooked the drive. Kelly glanced casually out, and her eyes widened in astonishment.

A yellow compact stood in front of the house. It had obviously just arrived—a man in blue overalls was getting out and looking around, clearly intending to call at the door.

Impulsively, Kelly threw open the window and leaned out.

'Don't knock,' she called in a conspiratorial tone. 'They're all asleep. Is that my car?'

He consulted his documents. 'Miss Francis? Sure, this is your compact. They said you wanted it early, that right?'

'Yes, it's fine. Is there anything to sign? Can you wait a moment till I come down?' Delighted, she retreated and scrambled into jeans and a blue shirt. They'd promised the car before breakfast, but she'd forgotten all about it. Leaving her feet bare, she ran softly down the stairs and opened the front door. No Joss Varney to block her way this time! It took only moments to sign the documents and accept the keys; she had already arranged to take the delivery man into Carmel and pay at the office.

'Off on holiday?' the delivery man said, grinning at her. 'Where are you going?'

Kelly opened her mouth to say she didn't know, but found herself saying, 'King's Canyon. I want to see the sequoias.'

He nodded. 'It's great up there. Still quite a bit of snow too, I wouldn't wonder. Hear they had a few spring blizzards out that way last week.'

Kelly thanked him and closed the door. Now for her escape! It shouldn't take long—her clothes were still half packed. She could be on her way before anyone else woke, out of the reach—and the clutches—of Joss Varney for ever.

But she had reckoned without Shona. As she turned from the front door, the housekeeper's figure appeared from the kitchen. And Kelly stood looking at her, washed with guilt and unable to think of a thing to say.

'Did I hear right, Miss Kelly?' Shona moved towards her. 'Are you leaving us so suddenly?'

Kelly nodded. 'I have to, Shona.'

The old woman studied her for a moment, then sighed. 'Aye. It's no' been easy for you—I can see that. But it's a great shame, for all that.' She turned away. 'You'll take a bit of breakfast before you go.'

Kelly hesitated. She hated hurting Shona—but she had to get away before Joss woke up. 'Could you give me something to take with me?' she asked, and Shona nodded.

'I'll make it up right away.' She turned back and touched Kelly on the arm. 'I don't mind telling you, Miss Kelly, I'm disappointed,' she said earnestly. 'I thought, when I looked out that first day and saw him standing there with you in his arms—well, you'll know what I thought. But that other one—there's always trouble where she's about.' She pursed her lips and shook her head sadly. 'Well, I'll away into my kitchen and make you a snack. Just don't go off without it, now.'

'Thank you, Shona. You've been good to me.' On impulse, Kelly leaned forward and kissed the dry cheek. 'I'll send you a postcard from King's Canyon!' And she turned and ran hurriedly up the stairs.

The house was still quiet as Kelly thrust the
last of her cases into the car and scrambled in,
taking the breakfast-pack from Shona. She sat
for a moment taking a last, lingering look at
Pacific Glade. A lot seemed to have happened
since she had first come here. She would miss
it. It was a place in which she could have been
happy.

But there was no turning back now. After last
night, she knew that she dared not stay another
moment in the beautiful house that overlooked the
restless Pacific. She had to be gone—the faster,
and the farther, the better.

She nodded to the delivery man, who had
offered to get the unfamiliar car up to the road
for her, and they were away.

The early morning roads were quiet as Kelly
drove cautiously through the streets of Carmel.
She felt some regret at leaving the pretty little
town. There was so much here still to see—Big
Sur, the national park down the coast with its
inland cliff scenery; Pacific Grove, where the
great butterflies made their annual migration to
cluster on the trees; the Carmel Mission, with its
Spanish-style buildings; Monterey itself, with its
sweeping blue bay, Fisherman's Wharf and
Cannery Row.

But she would be back, she promised herself.
At the end of her tour, when she returned the car,
she would have a few days here then, pottering
around. Maybe Joss would have gone back to his
gold-dredging by then, or even to Seattle. In any

case, there would be no reason why he should find out she was here.

Meanwhile, she was heading for a completely different scene, a place that would wipe all thoughts of Pacific Glade and the turmoil she had gone through there, clean from her mind.

After a while she paused to look at the maps provided with the car and work out a route. She was aware that, once heading the wrong way along a freeway, it might be many miles before she could change direction. She tore a page from her diary and scribbled down road numbers and the names of towns she must pass through. Then, overlooking the sparkling waters of the Bay, she ate some of the food Shona had given her.

The drive was interesting from the start, and Kelly made a conscious effort to take note of the scenery she passed through, hoping that this would take her mind off the pain she was already beginning to feel at the thought of never seeing Joss again. It's no good thinking that way, she told herself fiercely—he's no good to you, no good at all. And she stared ahead, concentrating on the road and the acres of globe artichokes that seemed to be the main crop around Monterey, stretching as far as the eye could see. Beside the road, on the verges, were more of the ice-plants that also typified this region, together with bright orange Californian poppies.

Overhead, she caught occasional glimpses of huge black birds that circled incessantly—turkey vultures, Joss had called them. And smaller birds darted in front of her—black birds with bright red wingtips, blue jays and many others she had no hope of identifying.

The journey was, she calculated, about two hundred miles. Not far on the straight, empty roads that patterned this part of California. Even with a fifty-five mile an hour speed limit, it shouldn't take too long. With no need to hurry, then, she could relax for the first time in days and begin to enjoy her holiday.

But that, she discovered, wasn't so easy. Try as she would, the thought of Joss Varney kept creeping into her mind. Was he awake yet? Was he up? Had he discovered her defection?

Irritably, Kelly shrugged her shoulders. She'd made up her mind to forget Joss, hadn't she? Well then—forget him!

She was now approaching hills and looked about her with delight. The artichokes had given way to the vines of wine-making country; now she was coming into rolling green hills and wooded pastures that strongly resembled parts of Wales. It was agricultural country, too—sheep and lambs grazed the fields, and she recognised with pleasure herds of brown, white-faced Hereford cattle. As she drew higher into the hills, the terrain became wilder, with the occasional crag rising above the winding river beside the road. The road twisted higher and higher, each bend bringing fresh delight, and suddenly the view to her right opened out and she found herself staring over a huge lake.

'Oh—beautiful!'

The cry broke unbidden from her lips as she drove on, gazing with pleasure at the lake. All round, the hills swept down to the water, forming creeks and bays; the sparkling wavelets were alive with motor cruisers and sailing boats, their sails brilliant splashes of colour against the blue. Around the strands, she could see picnic parties; there was an occasional flash of white foam as a water-skier zoomed by.

At this point, Kelly saw a small complex of buildings. Beyond them was a strange device, looking for all the world like a giant eggbeater, and as her brows creased she realised that the lake was in fact a reservoir—the San Luis Reservoir, it said on the notices—and that visitors were welcome to come and look around the centre.

Well, she had plenty of time, and this *was* a holiday. Why not? And Kelly swung the little car off the highway and brought it to a halt in the car park.

It was late in the afternoon when Kelly, uncomfortably aware that she had spent far too long at San Luis, started the car again and continued with her journey. She had never intended to stay so long, she reflected, bidding a reluctant goodbye to the great reservoir. In fact, she had now left herself with barely enough time to reach her destination before dark. But the break had done her good, there was no doubt of it. And without the few hours' refreshing sleep in the secluded hollow she had found to have lunch, she might well have had an accident later on.

The guide at the reservoir had been interesting and informative, and not only about the reservoir itself—before letting Kelly go to see the film in the tiny cinema, he had discoursed lengthily on English history, displaying a wider knowledge of past kings and queens than Kelly had possessed even at school. The film itself, a rundown on the Californian reservoirs, had been fascinating. And afterwards she had walked the short distance to see the new Darrius Rotor, which she had likened to a huge eggbeater. It was in fact, the guide had explained, a wind-powered generator and had only recently been erected as an experiment in feeding electricity gained in this manner into the grid system. 'Free power, you see,' he had told her. 'Of course, it has to be wound up to get it started, but once that's done and there's a good wind blowing—and that's most of the time up here—why, it just goes on. Might be you'll be seeing a lot more of them in a few years' time.'

Then Kelly had returned to the car and fetched the rest of the food that Shona had provided, taking it to a quiet hollow overlooking the reservoir. And there, suddenly overwhelmingly sleepy after her restless night and early start, she had fallen asleep.

Well, it didn't really matter, provided the Snow Lodge Motel could put her up. And to make sure, she telephoned before leaving the reservoir and booked a room. That done, she set off again with an easy mind.

Joss would certainly know she had gone now.

He might have remained in ignorance until almost lunchtime—even longer if he had gone out—but by then he would surely have become suspicious. And Shona would, of course, have to confirm what had happened. Well, none of it mattered any more, Kelly reminded herself without much conviction. She was out of his clutches, as she should have been the very first day he took her there. Why she had stayed, she couldn't imagine. It had only caused turmoil and heartbreak.

But now she was away. And she had to start getting over him.

With a deliberate effort, Kelly turned her mind again to the scenery she was passing through. The hills were behind her now and she was once more travelling across plains, this time planted with orange groves; miles and miles of dark green trees with the ripe fruit glowing like lanterns in their branches. She even saw one or two notices inviting her to pick her own oranges, a sight which took her straight back to the fruit-farming areas of England. And at one small settlement, she stopped and bought a huge bag of the luscious fruit for a dollar, marvelling at their cheapness and wondering if she would ever be able to get through them all.

The hours passed. She turned off Highway 99 at Fresno and took the 180 for King's Canyon. There had been a good deal of traffic as she passed through the busy highways of Fresno, much of it composed of people going home from work, but now the road was quieter and she kept up a steady rate of progress. The sun had almost gone as she approached the first grassy foothills of the sierra, but she wasn't too worried; the mountains of the National Park were clearly visible now, and with her room safely booked it didn't really matter whether she arrived before dark or not.

She drove on. The road was very lonely now, with only an occasional farmhouse glimpsed across the fields, its lights winking in the dusk. Once or twice she passed a wayside cafe, but they were few and far apart. She hoped that the car wouldn't break down—goodness knows when she could have got help. But the little compact kept steadily on, taking her through the rounded hills into the last stretch of plain before the sierra itself.

It was almost fully dark when she passed through Squaw Valley and thankfully filled her tank with petrol. The trading post was open here, and there was a motel too. Kelly wondered briefly whether to cancel her room at the Snow Lodge for tonight and stay here instead, going on the next day. But it would surely only take an hour or so to get there now, she thought impatiently.

Joss would quite certainly know now that she had gone. What would be his reaction? Fury, she guessed, because she had dared not only to refuse his offer of marriage—if it had ever been serious—but also to escape, to leave without his express permission.

The sheer effrontery of the man still left her gasping! To *kidnap* her in the way that he had—

there really wasn't any other word for it. To force her to stay at his house, though just how he had achieved that was now vague in her mind. And then, after flaunting his ex-mistress in front of her for a whole day, to suggest marriage—and marriage of a kind that revolted her. A marriage based entirely on lust—hers as well as his, she had to admit though the knowledge made her squirm—and designed entirely to suit his own purposes.

Thank goodness the car had arrived early that morning! Thank goodness she had had the sense to override the demands of her body and make her escape.

The road climbed steeply, winding tortuously as it made its way up the sharp escarpment. The motel stood at about seven thousand feet, Kelly knew, so there was a good deal of climbing to do. She wished now that she hadn't slept so long at San Luis. It was no fun negotiating these sharp twists and turns plus the steep gradient, in darkness.

She was also uncomfortably aware of the increasing height of the cliffside up which the road was winding, and its closeness to the edge of the road. If she took her eyes from the road for a second, she could see lights winking on the plain far—too far—below. Hastily, she jerked her gaze back to the road ahead and wished fervently that she had someone with her to share the journey and ease her increasing tension.

The first vestiges of snow had begun to appear

at the sides of the road when she became aware of someone behind her.

At first she thought she was imagining it. The lights of the other car lit up the road ahead only briefly before she swung again into yet another tight corner. But as it drew closer she began to find comfort in its presence. The idea of possible danger to her from the occupant on this lonely road didn't occur to her. She was too glad to have the presence of another human being at least within sight.

The unknown car was close behind her now, and she knew a sharp disappointment as it took advantage of a rare straight stretch of road to overtake her. As it passed, she saw that it was a larger car than her own, a sleek grey model and obviously capable of climbing the escarpment much more efficiently than her small compact. So she was to be left alone again, she thought dolefully, watching it draw ahead. Well, at least it proved that other people did come up here at night!

But the other driver must have realised her inexperience and nervousness. Instead of vanishing into the night, the grey car stayed ahead of her; just close enough for her to be able to follow it comfortably round each twist and turn. Its powerful lights beamed strongly up the road, lighting up the trees and rocks on her left, the ridge of snow that marked the cliff edge on her right.

It was not until they were inside the National

Park that Kelly realised that the other driver must be making for the Snow Lodge too. And as she followed him gratefully along the last stretch of road, between high banks of snow, and into the wide space in front of the motel, she determined to thank him before she did anything else at all.

The two cars halted side by side. Kelly closed her eyes for a moment, mentally, emotionally and physically exhausted. Then she clicked open her seat-belt, opened the car door and slid out.

The other driver was already out of his car. In the darkness, and half blinded with weariness, Kelly took little notice of his appearance. She went over to him, holding her hands out in grati- tude.

'Thank you so much for guiding me up that last stretch! I've never driven up such a steep, twisting road before—I think if you hadn't been there I'd have probably gone over the edge, through sheer fright!'

'Well, that wouldn't have done,' a familiar, deep voice remarked. 'It wouldn't have done at all—especially when it's taken me all day to catch up with you!'

Kelly gasped and recoiled. The looming bulk of Joss Varney moved from the shadows into the light cast by the windows of the motel and, before she could escape, he laid his hand on her arm. Kelly jerked with dismay, then stood still. What was the use of trying? She could never, never escape this man. And here, at the end of the road into the King's Canyon Park, with snow and darkness all round them, they might as well have been on the edge of the world. There was nowhere else to run to.

'Come on,' Joss said grimly. 'Get your things and we'll go inside. Just in case you've forgotten, we've still got that unfinished business to settle!'

CHAPTER TEN

MOVING like an automaton, Kelly allowed him to lead her into the motel. She watched dully while he confirmed the reservation and took the key, noted with detachment that nobody seemed at all surprised that Miss Francis was now accompanied by Mr Varney and apparently sharing a room with him. It all seemed to be out of her control now. She stood like one in a dream, waiting for the whole incomprehensible thing to be over so that she could wake up.

'Hey,' said Joss, catching sight of her white face. 'You're just about all in. Look, you go over by the fire and have a look at the menu. I'll take our things up, then we'll have supper. Have you eaten anything at all today?'

The motel was a trading store and restaurant as well, with tables set round the cedar-clad room before a huge log fire. Kelly stumbled over to it and sank into a chair, looking without much interest at the menu. She must be hungry, she supposed, but at the moment she was numb of all sensation.

Joss returned and she looked at him warily. His dark hair tangled on his brow, but otherwise he looked fresh and as in command of the situation as ever. He was wearing a thick sweater which he

took off when he saw that Kelly had chosen to sit
near the fire; under it he wore a close-fitting dark
blue shirt and slacks. The gold of his watch
gleamed on his wrist.

'We'll eat first,' he said in a tone that brooked
no argument, 'and talk later.'

'There's nothing to talk about,' Kelly muttered,
dragging together a shred of rebellion, and she
saw his lips tighten.

'If I say we talk,' he murmured in that silky voice
that spelt danger; 'we talk. I didn't come all the
way up here to be sent back with a flea in my ear.
So get this into your head. If we never speak to
each other again after tomorrow, we talk tonight.
All night if necessary.'

A tiny spark of mutiny stirred in Kelly at that,
but she was too fatigued to say anything. She
watched without much interest as Joss ordered a
meal, then sipped at her coffee which was brought
immediately and began to feel a little better. By
the time she had drunk a very good soup and
managed most of a sizeable pizza and salad, her
strength was beginning to return and, with it, her
confused feelings about Joss Varney.

When he finally indicated that it was time to go
to their room, therefore, she was ready for him.

The room was at the back of the motel, reached
by covered outside steps and a verandah that ran
the length of the accommodation. It was strikingly
beautiful in the moonlight, with deep snow still
surrounding the building and wooden chalets
dotted about amongst the trees. In any other cir-

cumstances, Kelly would have been thrilled at the idea of spending a night here. But now. . . She watched helplessly as Joss unlocked the door which formed part of the huge glass wall of the room, and slid it back, motioning her inside. Then she held out her hand.

'Thank you,' she said formally. 'I enjoyed the meal and I feel a lot better now. Perhaps I'll see you in the morning—or are you leaving now?'

Joss stared at her. 'Leaving? I'm not leaving— not tonight. Not until I've got things sorted out with you for once and for all.' He grasped her wrist in his familiar cruel grip. 'Now stop play-acting, Kelly, and come inside. I've had just about enough of your tricks, I'm telling you, and if you try on anything more I won't be answerable for the consequences.'

Kelly bit her lip. He had won, and they both knew it. That didn't mean she was going to give in all the way along the line. But there was nothing she could do about his presence now.

Joss stood aside and she went into the room. The luxury of it caught her by surprise; somehow in this remote place, she had expected rougher accommodation. But the room, even with its glass wall, was cosy and warm, heated by an electric fire. Underfoot was thick carpet; the huge double bed was flanked by large lamps, there was a desk and a dressing-table, and in the far corner stood a round table, with two comfortable-looking armchairs beside it. A door opposite led into the bathroom, with its spotlessly clean shower compartment.

She'd certainly been to some nice places with Joss Varney, Kelly reflected with some bitterness. It was a pity the atmosphere between them didn't match up to the beauty of their surroundings.

'Right.' Joss closed and locked the glass door behind him and drew across the heavy curtain, cutting out the view of darkness and snow and enclosing them in a world of intimate comfort. 'Now we'll talk.'

'Talk?' she queried bitterly. 'Just what is there to talk about? I would have thought we'd said enough—too much, if anything.'

He stood with his back to the curtains, his eyes sombre.

'In a sense, you're right. We've spent our time saying all the wrong things to each other. Things we didn't mean—things——'

'Speak for yourself!' she interrupted furiously. 'I meant every word *I* said, every single one.'

He sighed. 'And here we go again. Look, Kelly, if we're ever to get this mess sorted out, you've got to keep a hold on yourself. O.K., O.K., you don't need to say it—I've got to keep myself in check too. And that's not easy, I can tell you, so let's make a bargain, shall we—I will if you will! How's that?'

In spite of herself, Kelly smiled. The tense atmosphere lightened a little and she dropped into one of the armchairs. The double bed stood between them, but for the present, she knew instinctively, it did not present a threat. Though it might be a different story later, and she shivered, but whether in fear or anticipation she was unable to tell.

Joss came round the bed and drew the other armchair close so that he sat facing her. He leaned forward and took her hands in his, and Kelly's spine tingled.

'How did you find out I was coming here?' she asked in a low voice.

'Shona told me. Oh, she didn't want to at first, I had to talk to her for a long time before she gave in.' His grin was rueful. 'It's the first time Shona's ever gone against me, and it came as a bit of a shock, I can tell you. Made me think a bit differently—about the way I've been behaving towards you in particular.'

Kelly gave a silent cheer for Shona, while reserving judgment as to whether the Scotswoman had been wise in giving her away.

'I sure didn't expect to come across you on that road in the dark, though,' he went on. 'I thought you'd be here way before this, though I knew you hadn't arrived when I telephoned mid-afternoon. What happened to you?'

Kelly explained about her visit to San Luis and he nodded. 'I didn't get a lot of sleep myself, until just after dawn. Then I went out like a light and didn't know anything until nearly lunchtime.' He touched her cheek. 'Poor Kelly! You must be flaked—but I'm not taking any more chances. We get this over *now*, before you slip through my fingers again.'

Kelly shivered again at his touch. Don't let him kiss me again, she prayed—oh, don't. For if he did, she knew that this time she would be lost. Here in the snug room in the mountains, with deep snow outside and the night before them, Joss had her in the palm of his hand. The question was—did he know it?

'There are quite a lot of things I want to tell you,' he was saying, 'but first I have to get the past out of the way. My past—my marriage, in fact.'

'You don't have to tell me anything,' Kelly whispered, but he corrected her grimly.

'But I do. And you have to listen, if you never listen to me again. I can't let this end without getting the truth out in the open between us. Get that?'

There was a pause, then he went on. 'Cassie was just a kid when we got married. Oh, she'd been around, she knew the world—but she was a kid for all that. And I guess I wasn't much better, or I wouldn't have forced the pace as I did. I was crazy about her, you see—head-over-heels crazy in love with her. I just had to have her.'

Don't go on, Kelly begged silently, her nerves screaming. She didn't want to hear this, didn't want to feel the jealousy burning through her as Joss talked about his love for Cassie. Hadn't he tortured her enough?

'Well, it didn't work out. Anyone could have told me it wouldn't. Not that I'd have listened. I've always been bullheaded.' He paused and

Kelly stole a glance at him, shocked to find that his eyes were shadowed with pain. 'After a year or so Cassie started playing the field again. We were up in Seattle at the time. I was busy—I was working my way up in the firm, trying to make my place—my dad didn't believe in nepotism and if I hadn't made it by my own efforts, someone else would be running the outfit now. So there was Cassie, with too much free time—young, beautiful and bored. Ready to enjoy herself. And enjoy herself she did.'

His voice was bitter now and Kelly, feeling that he needed her to say something, whispered: 'You mean, she—she found someone else?'

'She sure did. And more than one, too. Even after she became pregnant—for a while.' His words came slowly, with a difficulty born of many years' reticence. 'And then the baby was born, prematurely, too weak to live for more than a week or so, and Cassie died.'

Impulsively, Kelly clasped his hands between her own. 'But that wasn't your fault,' she exclaimed, sensing the blame he still heaped on himself. 'Nobody could have helped that.'

'It shouldn't have happened,' he said harshly. 'It wouldn't have, if I hadn't married her.'

Kelly was silent, thinking over the tragic little story. But the baby, she wanted to cry. What about the baby? Did he *have* to die? Couldn't he have been helped to live, to grow up, to live some kind of life, however delicate he might have been?

'I guess you know about the kid,' he said

heavily. 'Damask told you—yes, she admitted it when she saw I was determined to come after you. Only the way she told it, it didn't show me up in any too good a light, I guess.'

Kelly bit her lip. At that moment it hit her that Damask's version of the story had been wildly exaggerated. The baby had been premature, too weak to survive—but nothing worse than that. How could Damask have invented such a wicked story! Her voice quivered as she said: 'But why—why let him die? That poor little baby—didn't he have a right to live? Even if he was never to be strong——'

'You don't know the facts, Kelly,' he said in a voice that silenced her. 'There was nothing anyone could do to save Robert, Kelly. And believe me, I didn't spare any expense to see that everything possible was done. He had the best care the States could provide. But I guess he was just too small and too weak to survive.' And then, after a long pause, he added in a voice so low that Kelly could barely hear him: 'I never even saw him, you know. Cassie wouldn't let me—wouldn't let me see her either. Because—and nobody else knows this, Kelly—Robert wasn't my son.'

The words dropped like stones into the utter peace of the room. Their eyes held for a long moment, then Kelly found her voice.

'He—he wasn't your son?'

'No. When Cassie found she was pregnant, I was away in Alaska—where I'd been for nearly three months. He couldn't possibly have been mine—though for her sake, I pretended I'd flown down secretly for a night to see her. But by the time we got to that stage it was too late for poor Robert. She'd tried to get rid of him, you see— tried every method she could think of. That's why he was premature.'

Tears filled Kelly's eyes. No wonder Joss had been embittered. No wonder he'd become cynical, hostile, interested only in making money.

'There's just one more thing,' he said quietly. 'That gold—the devil's gold, you called it—that I spend three months a year dredging out of the river. It all goes to a children's home up in Seattle. I founded it in memory of Cassie and Robert. Oh, it needs more money than the gold fetches, but it helps me to feel I'm doing something *myself*—not just dipping my hand into a well-lined pocket. It's my way of—well, of saying sorry, I suppose. There doesn't seem to be anything else I can do.'

The room swayed around Kelly. So she'd been wrong all along the line. She'd misjudged Joss Varney in every possible way. She knew now that here was a man saddened beyond tolerance by a tragedy that was none of his fault. A man who desperately needed love, reassurance, comfort. Did it matter any more that he didn't love her? What possible right had she to *expect* him to love her—yet? Maybe he would never be able to bring himself to love again. But somehow she had to make him see that she was aware of the wrong she'd done him—and there was only one way she knew of doing that.

With a little cry she was in his arms, and she felt the groan burst from his chest as he enfolded her close against him. Her heart thudded as their lips met in a long hungry kiss. Then she flung back her head as his lips left hers to travel down the slim column of her neck, resting for a moment on the pulse that beat in the hollow of her throat, while one hand slid round to cover her breast. The buttons of her shirt parted under his onslaught and her breast sprang into his hand, taut and swollen with desire; with a muffled gasp, he lifted her in his arms and laid her on the bed, burying his face in her breasts while she ran her hands through the tangle of his hair and pressed her body against him.

'Kelly,' he muttered, sliding his hands under her shirt and slipping it from her shoulders. 'Kelly—there's still something we've got to get straight. . . .'

Tenderly, she slid her hands down his chest, undoing buttons as she went and pulling his shirt from his waistband. 'It doesn't matter,' she whispered. 'Nothing matters—now.'

'But it does!' Making a superhuman effort, he rolled away from her, his eyes agonised. 'I want you, Kelly—you know that. Dammit, I've wanted you since that first moment when I saw you in 'Frisco airport. It was hell, knowing you still belonged to Mark—and it's been hell ever since. Except,' and his eyes softened, 'for one or two glimpses of heaven. ... Look, you've got to understand. The way I proposed to you last night—it wasn't meant to be like that.' As if he couldn't resist it, he slid a hand from her throat to her knee, drawing from her a long shudder of delight and longing. 'Damn you, Kelly, when I'm with you I can't think straight—I can't talk straight. Everything comes out wrong and before I know it, we're fighting again.'

'We're not fighting now.' Kelly wriggled close to him again, letting her own hands roam so that he closed his eyes and moved sensuously.

'No, we're not fighting,' he growled, pulling her tightly against him. 'But this isn't much better, is it—I still can't think straight. Look, Cat's Eyes—be still a moment—I've got to say this and it's damned well not easy. I haven't said it to anyone since—since before Cassie died—Kelly, I *love* you, don't you understand? You've got into my heart, into my blood, you're the part I've been missing all these years. That's why I've got to marry you—those other reasons, they were just talk, just that damned silly defence I still had to put up. But I don't need to do that any more. I love you, and I want you with me for always—my wife, my lover, my mate in everything I do. Do you get that?' He raised himself on one elbow and stared down at her, his eyes dark with urgency.

'And Damask?' she whispered, hardly daring to ask the question but knowing that nothing must now be allowed to stand between them.

'Damask!' He gave a short bark of laughter. 'Damask is a very calculating lady—you must have realised that. O.K., she got me out of the

morass after Cassie died—showed me there were
still things to live for. I suppose I'll always be
grateful for that. But not because she was anybody
special—she just happened to be there. I soon
realised we weren't on any sort of wavelength, not
really. That's when she took off and married
Bentley, and I was glad to see her go.'

'But—yesterday?' Kelly faltered. 'I thought—
from the way you behaved——'

'Oh, Kelly,' he said, and all the mockery had
gone from his voice now. 'Don't you realise? I
was mad with jealousy over Stuart—I just had to
get back at you some way.' He grinned suddenly.
'Maybe it wasn't quite fair on Damask—she
didn't take it too kindly when she cottoned on.
But she'll get over that.'

Kelly's hands, which had been gently stroking
his body, dropped away. She lay under him,
looking deep into the brown eyes that watched
her with such intensity, no longer veiled so that
now she could see there everything she had
yearned for. She saw a deep, abiding and passionate love; a love that could satisfy her all the days
of her life. A love such as she had only dreamed
of.

'Oh, Joss,' she whispered at last as relief and
pure happiness warmed her body. 'Joss, I love
you—I love you with all my heart.'

She touched his face gently, wonderingly,
stroking away the harsh lines of bitterness for
ever. Just at this moment, it seemed incredible
that she and Joss could ever have fought. And if a

tiny voice, somewhere at the back of her mind, told her that they would certainly fight again, every bit as tempestuously as they had in the past, she smiled in the knowledge that their fights would be merely a prelude and stimulation to lovemaking. They would always have the means to make up.

And on that thought, desire flooded her body again. She raised her eyes and saw the same look in Joss's. They drew together in a simultaneous movement, and when he claimed her lips once more she responded with love and joy and total abandon.

'Suppose we get under the sheets?' he murmured as he unzipped her jeans and slid them down her legs. 'I don't want you getting cold, my love.'

'I'll never be cold with you to warm me,' she murmured. But she went under the sheets with him; and as they lay together, naked and entwined, she knew that she had reached at last the haven she had been seeking. Exultantly, she gave her body up to the fierce and passionate lovemaking in which she and Joss matched so well. And then all conscious thought ceased. There was nothing left but the rapture of true fulfilment.

Fall in love with Mills & Boon

Do you remember the first time you fell in love? The heartache, the excitement, the happiness? Mills & Boon know – that's why they're the best-loved name in romantic fiction.

The world's finest romance authors bring to life the emotions, the conflicts and the joy of true love, and you can share them – between the covers of a Mills & Boon.

We are offering you the chance to enjoy ten specially selected Mills & Boon Romances absolutely FREE and without obligation. Take these free books and you will meet ten women who must face doubt, fear and disappointment before discovering lasting love and happiness.
